'It feels as if I've **** a long, long t strange voice.

'Somehow. . . But. . took a step back.

Meg gasped, and took a step back as well, and stood staring up at him in the moonlight. Their eyes locked.

And it was just as Rob had said. It was as. . .as if there was something between them that had always been there, and always would.

And it scared Meg to death!

Marion Lennox has had a variety of careers—medical receptionist, computer programmer and teacher. Married, with two young children, she now lives in rural Victoria, Australia. Her wish for an occupation which would allow her to remain at home with her children and her dog led her to begin writing, and she has now published a number of medical romances.

Recent titles by the same author:

BRIDAL REMEDY
PRESCRIPTION—ONE BRIDE
PRESCRIPTION—ONE HUSBAND

PROMISE OF
A MIRACLE

BY
MARION LENNOX

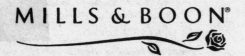

MILLS & BOON®

*All the characters in this book have no existence outside the imagina-
tion of the author, and have no relation whatsoever to anyone bearing
the same name or names. They are not even distantly inspired by any
individual known or unknown to the author, and all the incidents are
pure invention.*

*First published in Great Britain 1997
Harlequin Mills & Boon Limited,
Eton House, 18-24 Paradise Road, Richmond, Surrey TW9 1SR*

© Marion Lennox 1997

ISBN 0 263 80203 5

*Set in Times 10 on 11 pt. by
Rowland Phototypesetting Limited
Bury St Edmunds, Suffolk*

03-9707-50595-D

*Printed and bound in Great Britain
by Mackays of Chatham PLC, Chatham*

PROLOGUE

DR ROB DANIELS, veterinary surgeon and part-time farmer, reined in his horse and surveyed his domain with the air of a man at peace. The afternoon sun was glinting on the sea before him. The beach spread out on either side of man and horse as golden ribbons of sand stretching to the horizon. Too distant to intrude on this idyllic setting, the town of Gundowring was a distant smudge on the far headland—a faint cluster of buildings shrouded by the gentle sea mist.

In the paddocks around him Rob's cattle were grazing in placid contentment, and the surgery bell hadn't pealed for over three hours. Three blessed hours. . .

Three hours of peace on a Saturday afternoon was an almost unheard-of luxury for a vet on call for the entire district, and for Rob these three hours marked the start of his healing. Until now he'd worked in a kind of limbo, hoping desperately that one day he could break free from the shrouds of his past. Today. . . Today for the first time he felt that he could finally emerge.

He should go in and do some paperwork, Rob told himself. He didn't. Rob stayed where he was, a man who seemed part of this farm—of his land, his horizons and the animals he loved so much. This farm he'd missed for so long.

He should go in—but, despite his new-found peace, there was a trickle of premonition running down Rob's spine which told him that he should soak in this stillness. His premonition told him that somewhere. . .somewhere not too far away. . .something was happening that might well disturb this fragile peace for ever. . .

CHAPTER ONE

THE dog hit the car with a thud that made the small
sedan jerk sideways.

Meg braked to a halt. She closed her eyes as the car
stopped, trying to block out that last awful image—and
then finally recovered enough to look to Eve. The child
in the passenger seat was staring straight ahead, and what
colour had been in the thirteen-year-old's gaunt cheeks
was completely gone.

Dear heaven, they didn't need this.

The bad fairy looking over these two girls was certainly doing her best to make this trip a nightmare. How
would Eve's fragile emotional state handle a dog crushed
by a car?

And what. . .? Meg swallowed as she looked across at
her cousin's white face. What if the dog was still alive?

The small animal had come from nowhere, hurtling
out of the surrounding bush as if pursued by demons and
giving Meg nowhere to dodge. The tiny scrap of black
and white fur had disappeared almost as Meg had seen
it, and then the thud. . .

The thud meant that it had definitely been hit. The
thud meant that Meg must now lift a lifeless dog from
the road. While Eve watched. . .

'Stay in the car,' Meg whispered.

Eve didn't move and Meg put a hand out to touch
the young girl's arm. 'It's OK, Eve. We're fine. It was
just. . .'

'A dog. I saw.' Eve's voice was almost uninterested.

Oh, help. . .

It wasn't fear of facing a dead or dying dog that made

Meg cringe now. After two years of medical residency in the casualty ward of St Mark's Meg had grown to believe herself almost immune to horror. But Eve. . .

Meg couldn't think of Eve now. She had to cope with the dog.

'Stay in the car, Eve,' Meg repeated heavily, thrusting away the grimness of the girl's expression as she pushed open the car door. She closed the door behind her, hoping that Eve wouldn't be able to see what was outside. Somewhere under the wheels was something she'd rather not face herself. And finally she knelt on the roadside to look.

The dog was still alive.

The small animal was lying on its side on the gravel deep beneath the car. It was gloomy underneath, compared to the harsh glare of Australian sun above the car, but as Meg's eyes grew accustomed to the dimness she could make out enough to sense life.

Enough to see there was an eye looking at her—an eye embedded within a limp and apparently lifeless bunch of fur.

The staring eye was all that Meg could see, but suddenly her emotions were overwhelming. Meg might tell herself that she was immune to horror but such a statement was far from the truth. She'd hurt this little animal. She'd been talking to Eve. Talking at Eve. Worrying about Eve. If she'd been concentrating. . .

Meg's voice trembled in a frightened whisper. 'Oh, dear heaven, I'm sorry. . .I'm so sorry. . .'

This wasn't Dr Meg Preston speaking, twenty-eight years old and an efficient medical practitioner accustomed to years of dealing with road trauma. This was a frightened girl who'd taken a difficult burden on her shoulders for far too long, and was now finding it almost enough to crush her. To Meg's dismay, she felt the beginnings of tears prick behind her eyes, and she fought them back with an almost Herculean effort.

The little dog still didn't move.

If the dog was so badly hurt that it couldn't move. . . If its back was broken. . . Would she have to put it out of its pain?

Meg thought briefly of the sparse medical supplies she carried with her and she bit her lip in indecision. She had nothing she could use to put a dreadfully injured dog out of its suffering.

She was ahead of herself, she told herself savagely. First Meg had to lift the dog from under the car and see how badly it was hurt. Or drive the car clear. . .

The dog might well have been dead, for all it was moving. It seemed absolutely lifeless—except for that one wide eye. The eye rested on Meg, as if waiting.

The look in that pathetic eye stirred Meg to a decision. Helplessness receded as professional competence and years of training fell back into place. She wriggled forward.

Reaching in and pulling the little dog out was probably the wrong thing to do. Maybe she was asking to be bitten by a terrified, wounded animal, but there was something about this tiny dog that made Meg refuse to think of starting the car and driving it clear. The motor would terrify the dog more and, despite what had happened, there was something about the way the creature looked out at her that spoke of trust.

So Dr Meg Preston wriggled her slender body further under the car—slithering slowly through the dust so as not to frighten the injured animal further—and her hand reached out tentatively to feel.

'It's OK. It's OK, little one. I'm not about to hurt you more than I already have. It's OK.' Meg's voice was a low, monotonous whisper, designed to reassure. It was the voice she used to calm terrified children and it seemed to work just as well here as it did in Casualty. And slowly, slowly, Meg's fingers managed to touch.

The dog didn't flinch as Meg's hand felt its fur. Either it was completely paralysed or it was too terror-struck or pain-filled to move. The injured animal lay absolutely passive while Meg edged closer—until her face was only a foot from the dog and both her hands were free to feel.

How to examine a dog while lying face down in dirt under a car. . .

Meg did her best. Her fingers ran carefully over the small body with practised precision, feeling for the worst in the dim light. She was feeling for what she couldn't see. Feeling for a split abdomen—a crushed body that would mean she had no choice but to immediately end a life.

There was blood—plenty of it—warm and sticky on her fingers, but there was no massive damage. Maybe there were broken bones—there'd have to be after a thud like that—and maybe there were internal injuries, but it seemed that the car must have knocked the dog aside rather than run right over it.

Gently—infinitely gently—and mindful of the damage she could do by shifting broken bones, Meg edged her hands under the dog, forming a cradle with her palms. The pup was tiny—the size of a small terrier and so thin that it was a featherweight. Meg could support nearly all the fragile body on her hands. Then, with blood trickling down through her fingers, she dragged both herself and the dog back out from under the car.

As she wriggled out Meg felt the gravel grazing the bare skin of her legs and arms, but she couldn't use her hands to pull herself clear. Both hands were totally occupied with dog.

Eve was waiting.

Despite Meg's orders, Eve had climbed from the car and was standing on the grass verge. When she saw what Meg was dragging out the child flinched back in horror.

'Oh, no. . . Oh, Meg. . .' Eve knelt down in the dust

as if, despite her horror, she felt compelled to look.

And Meg's eyes flew to Eve with wonder. There was a gentleness in the child's voice and a concern that Meg hadn't heard for months. There was interest in the voice where for so long there'd been nothing but apathy.

'Oh, Meg, have we killed him?' Eve whispered.

Meg forced her eyes back to the dog, her mind racing. She'd been fighting for Eve's interest for so long—and to find it now for a dog so badly damaged. . .

'He's still alive,' she managed, 'but I don't know how badly he's hurt. Grab a towel from the back seat.'

To Meg's further surprise, Eve did just that, moving with a speed and decisiveness totally at odds with the indifferent child Meg knew.

While Eve was turned away Meg made a fast, cursory inspection of the small dog. One of its hind legs was hanging at a horrid angle, and its hind quarters were rubbed raw with the gravel. Still, the bleeding appeared to be slowing. Maybe. . .maybe the little creature was saveable. It was a he, Meg noted. Maybe he was saveable.

The creature was a stray, though. There was no doubting that. The dog was a shaggy, misbegotten composite of breeds, his long black and white coat matted with months of neglect and his sides cleaving to the ribcage as if he was very close to starvation. If the car hadn't hit this dog, Meg guessed, hunger would have killed him very soon.

A stray. . . A dog no one wanted and half-dead before she'd hurt him with her car. And still the dog followed Meg's every move with those wide, trusting eyes.

Eve was back swiftly, spreading the towel on the grass and watching with eyes that were almost as anxious as the dog's while Meg laid the little animal gently onto the soft fabric.

'What will we do, Meg? Do you think he lives around

here? Will we try to find where he lives or should we take him straight to the vet. . .?'

And then the child paused and looked up as another car came around the bend and pulled to a halt.

Meg rose in relief. The truck was battered, and the man climbing from it was obviously a farmer—a big, beefy man in his late fifties. A local. . . That's what she needed, Meg thought thankfully. Someone who could take responsibility from her.

'Hi,' Meg managed, fighting for some semblance of assurance as the man approached. She didn't have much. Meg wiped her bloody hands on her shorts and decided that she definitely couldn't shake hands with anyone. A 'Hi' would have to do.

'What's the problem?' The farmer was gruffly interested. His eyes ran over the small sedan with its hire-car label, and then over the two girls before him.

Meg didn't look exactly reputable, she thought ruefully as the man's eyes rested on her. She flushed a little with embarrassment. Her denim shorts and white blouse were now bloodstained and filthy, and she'd scratched herself on the gravel as she'd crawled under the car. Her shoulder-length brown curls were caked with dust. The dog's blood was on her hands and her own blood was on her legs.

And Eve. . . The farmer's eyes moved to Meg's frail cousin and his brow creased in concern.

'We hit a dog,' Meg said quickly, trying to deflect the comment on Eve's appearance which was starting to seem almost inevitable from anyone who met them— stranger or not. 'I wonder. . . Could you help us? We're just. . . We're just tourists here and we don't know what to do.'

The farmer's gaze shifted reluctantly from Eve to the injured dog, lying on the towel at the girls' feet. What he saw made his face tighten in disgust.

'Hell, you might have done a better job of it than that. Should'a killed it outright, that one, I reckon.'

'What. . .what do you mean?' Meg still spoke fast, aware of Eve stiffening at her side.

'I mean it's a stray. I live just down the road here and I've seen this dog before. Caught it at my poultry a few weeks back and let off a few rounds of shot at it. Missed, though.' He surveyed it with dislike. 'He didn't get any of my chooks but it doesn't mean he hasn't killed others. I've got the gun in the back of the truck. Want me to finish it off for you?'

'No!' Suddenly Eve moved, thrusting her childish body between farmer and dog. 'Don't you touch him,' she whispered. 'We just want you to tell us where the vet is. Meg, don't let him touch him.'

Eve had spoken more in the last few minutes than she'd spoken for weeks. Meg put a hand on the girl's arm, but Eve shook it off. She stood, glaring at the farmer as if her frail body really was capable of withstanding force.

'What? You're not going to save the blasted thing?' the farmer demanded incredulously, staring down at Eve in disbelief. 'What the hell for?' He turned to Meg, as if questioning her sanity.

And Meg flinched. Now what?

The most sensible proposal was to do just what this man suggested. A starving stray, so badly injured. . . What on earth could Meg or Eve do for such a one? Even if they nursed him back to health there was no escaping the fact that Meg and Eve were due to return to England at the end of the month. There was no way they could take care of it long term.

If they saved the dog now it would have to be put down later.

Meg turned to face Eve, but as she did she came to a decision. There were tears pouring down Eve's cheeks.

This was the first emotion she'd seen from Eve. . .

Meg couldn't end this by allowing the farmer to blast the dog's life away here in the dust. Who knew how Eve would react?

Meg couldn't begin to imagine. No. They'd find a local vet and hand the responsibility over to him.

'Please. . . Tell us where to find the nearest vet,' Meg said firmly, and Eve's face lightened with gratitude. The arm she'd shaken from Meg's grasp suddenly dropped down to Meg's side, and Eve's fingers linked with Meg's bloodstained ones. A show of solidarity. . .

'You don't want. . .' the farmer began but he was cut short by Eve.

'Yes, we do.' Eve's voice was no longer a whisper. It was loudly defiant with a child's aggression when she was sure the strength was on her side. 'You keep your rotten gun to yourself. If you hadn't tried to shoot him you might have found who owns him and this never would have happened to the poor little dog. Meg, can I pick him up?'

'If you're careful not to move his body more than you must,' Meg sighed. 'Keep him rigid, Eve, and hold him on your lap while I drive.' And then, as Eve stooped to collect her precious burden, Meg turned back to the farmer. 'Please, could you tell us where to find the vet?'

'But. . .'

'The vet will put him down if he needs to,' Meg said firmly, trying to put professional certainty into her voice. 'Thanks for your offer but I will take him to the vet.'

The farmer chewed his lip. One part of him wanted to use this opportunity to get rid of a nuisance, Meg could see. If they saved the creature and persuaded a neglectful owner to claim him the dog could be back, making trouble.

That wasn't Meg's problem. She fixed the farmer with a look of determination and waited.

And finally she had her answer.

'Doc Daniels lives on a farm up on the north headland at the end of this road,' the farmer said grudgingly, rubbing a work-coarsened finger on the side of his nose. 'It's a big white place, looking over the sea. You can't miss it and he's sometimes home Saturday afternoon. But, heck, miss. . .'

'I know,' Meg sighed. 'This isn't sensible. But sometimes. . .' She gently closed the car door on child and pup as Eve settled into the car's passenger seat with her precious burden. 'Sometimes when you have a thirteen-year-old you do the right thing as opposed to the sensible. It can't hurt.

'I hope it can't hurt,' she breathed to herself as she spoke to the farmer. 'I hope. . .

'Thank you for your help. . .' she started and made to leave, but she wasn't to get off quite so lightly.

'But, listen, what's wrong with the kid?' the farmer interrupted brusquely. 'She looks. . .'

'She looks fine.' Meg cut him off, hoping that Eve couldn't hear through the car door. 'Thank you again but we really do have to get this dog to the vet fast.'

And finally she escaped.

CHAPTER TWO

SURELY this wasn't the vet's surgery!

The house the farmer had directed them to was a farm-house set in one of the most wonderful places Meg could imagine. Gundowring was a fabulous district, anyway, but the vet surely had the pick of the properties. The house was set amongst a low, sprawling cluster of white-washed buildings built in stone and all facing the sea. The land was lushly green and undulating, with stands of ancient gums giving shade to cattle peacefully grazing in the late afternoon sun. There were no neighbouring houses within sight.

Meg bumped cautiously over the cattle grid, then parked outside the house. Leaving Eve and her wounded charge in the car, she walked through a mass of the native creamy-gold frangipani to the wide verandah surrounding the homestead.

A homestead, she thought. That's what this seems. A real Australian homestead. How could it be a vet's surgery?

It seemed, though, that the farmer had not misled her. A notice on the door told Meg she was at the right place.

For urgent veterinary attention please ring bell. Otherwise morning surgery starts at eight a.m. and I appreciate being undisturbed until then. Remember, a grumpy vet always charges more!

Despite her concerns, Meg grinned and sympathised. This man had his own methods of achieving a private life. Still, there was no way that Eve's dog could wait until morning. Reluctantly Meg put her hand on the bell and rang.

The bell system would have woken the dead. What happened made Meg almost jump from her skin. A bell pealed above her head and, as if in sympathetic detonation, a cacophony of bells sounded from each adjoining building.

They faded at last to silence—a silence fast replaced by dogs. From along the cliff came distant barking, rising to a crescendo as a pack of three Border collies came hurtling across the paddocks to investigate the intruder in their domain.

Followed by a man on a horse. . .

Meg walked to the edge of the verandah and watched him come.

A country vet. . . A professional colleague. . .

This was a man like no professional colleague Meg had met before.

In the distance the man seemed tall and loose-limbed, cantering across the paddocks on his magnificent chestnut stallion as if he'd been born on horseback. The man's work trousers and open-necked, short-sleeved shirt were serviceable, khaki. Apart from his clothes, though, the man seemed shaded to match his horse. His skin was bronzed with constant exposure to weather and his hair, tousled in the warm wind from the sea, was a rich red-brown with glints of gold.

As he rode nearer the man's features grew more impressive. He wasn't old, Meg thought—mid-thirties maybe, but no older. His strongly boned face and long frame seemed strengthened by bare, muscled arms and work-roughened hands. Man and horse emitted sheer, muscled power—as if this man worked the land as well as lived on it.

Meg took a step forward on the verandah toward the

approaching rider, and then she stopped. The man's eyes. . .

The man's eyes were a welcome in themselves as he swung down from the horse, clicked his dogs to heel and strode up the path to greet her. His deep-set eyes—a shade of green which was striking against his sun-browned skin—studied Meg with interest. The vet's generous mouth quirked into a smile of welcome and his smile. . . His smile almost held a challenge. Like a child daring another to crazy mischief. . .

This was crazy all by itself, Meg thought wildly. Meg's reaction was crazy.

Meg had been so angry at those who stared at Eve because of the child's physical appearance. And here was Meg, staring like a silly schoolgirl—all because this man was so darned good-looking that he almost took her breath away.

'What can I do to help you?'

Meg took a deep breath. The man's voice was some-how as Meg had expected—richly resonant and laced with the echo of the laughter in his eyes. The piercing green eyes ran over Meg's slim form as he grew closer. Meg knew she looked absolutely disreputable, with her hair tangled and matted with dust and her shorts and shirt liberally coated with blood. The man's smile slipped as concern took over. His stride quickened and he took the verandah steps three at a time.

'What's happened?'

'I hurt a dog.' To her fury, Meg's voice came out with a tremor. It seemed that the shock and strain of the last few hours—or maybe the strain of the last few months—was finally taking its toll. And this man heard it. He moved fast to reach her and strong hands came out to grasp Meg's arm as if he feared she'd fall.

'You hurt a dog?' The vet looked down into Meg's pale face, and then let his eyes fall further. Meg's blouse, where she'd held the dog, was soaked in blood and her bare legs were a mass of scratches. 'Are you hurt as well?' The humour was completely gone. There was only concern.

Dear heaven. . . This man was so big. The vet stood, looking down at her with such an expression that it was all Meg could do not to burst into tears. Here was a man of strength, willing to take her cares onto his broad shoulders. . .

Good grief! This was schoolgirl behaviour. Looking at a man like this. . .

Meg had left Paul back in England without a backward glance, assuring him that she could cope—and she could cope without a male! Of course she could. Her reaction now was just due to shock and fatigue. With a massive effort she managed to pull her arm from the man's concerned grasp.

'Y-yes. I'm sorry for. . .for worrying you.' Another deep breath. 'The blood's the dog's. Not mine. I hit him with the car. It's just. . .'

'It's a horrid feeling, hitting and injuring something,' the man told her gently, his eyes not leaving her face. 'No matter what it is. If I squash a frog on the road I feel bad, and a dog's so much worse. Where's the dog now?'

'In. . .in the car.' Meg knew that she sounded like a child—and that was just how this man was treating her. He looked out at her car as if he was surprised that Meg was old enough to drive.

'You brought him here? Is the dog yours, then?'

'No. I. . .we don't live here,' Meg faltered, moving off the verandah with him. The man took her arm again. He led her down the steps and out underneath the scented frangipani with a force that Meg was powerless to resist.

'Are you just passing through or here on holidays?' For all his polite enquiry the man was moving with speed, propelling Meg by his side down toward her car.

'I. . .we thought we might stop for a few days.'

'It's great place to stop. Gundowring's the best place to spend time this side of paradise.' He smiled. 'Now. . .' The vet paused as they reached the car, his eyes noting Eve's presence. He turned back to Meg, his eyes asking questions. Meg once more shook off the man's powerful hold and she pulled open the passenger door.

'Eve, this is the vet. I mean. . .' She cast a sudden, questioning glance up at the penetrating green eyes. 'I guess. . .I guess you are the vet?'

'I'm the vet,' the man agreed curtly, crouching on the grass beside the passenger door so that he could see the injured dog lying on Eve's lap. 'I'm Rob Daniels.'

He was no longer looking at Meg, and he wasn't seeing Eve.

This man must be the first person they'd met in months who hadn't stared straight at Eve and asked stupid questions or made a cruel comment. Instead, the man's eyes were all on the dog on Eve's lap, and before he'd finished speaking the vet's attention was totally focussed. His hands, with their strong, gentle fingers, were running lightly over the dog's frail form and he gave a soundless whistle.

'What have you got yourself into, mate?' he asked softly, and he was talking only to the dog. 'Don't you know you can't argue with cars? The damned things always win.'

Then there was complete silence as he carefully felt the dog all over.

Eve sat motionless and breathless as Rob Daniels made his careful examination of the dog on the child's lap. The dog also didn't move an inch. The creature lay absolutely submissively. They could do with him what they would, Meg thought bleakly. The pathetic little creature was totally in their hands.

At least the dog was no longer in Meg's hands, she thought with gratitude. The dog was now in the hands of this vet—or this man who looked more like a farmer than a vet. This veterinary surgeon with the kindly eyes and the gentle hands. It seemed no ghastly fate. At least. . .

'Will he. . .will he have to be put down?' Meg whispered at last, willing herself to ask the question. Seated behind her on the grass, the vet's three collies were watching with almost as much anxiety as Meg felt. It seemed that the whole world waited to hear what the vet would say.

Rob Daniels didn't answer immediately. Instead he ran his hand lightly down the dog's spine from head to tail—and then sat back a little.

'Has he moved at all?' he asked.

'No,' Meg told him. 'Do you think his back's broken?'

'His leg's certainly broken. I can't feel a break in the spinal cord, but it's possible. There's sensation, though. He reacted to my fingers. I can feel his tremor.' The vet frowned and then looked up to Eve's tear-stained face. 'Would you like to carry him into my surgery?' he asked Eve. 'If you'll bring him in I'll set up a drip straight away to counter the shock. We'll need X-rays before we know for sure what the damage is.'

Meg's eyes flew to Eve's face, and before the child could move she put a hand out to restrain her. 'No. Eve stays in the car.'

Meg's instinctive protest was made before she could stop herself and the vet rose and turned to her in surprise. His dark brows furrowed.

'Is there a problem?' he asked, and Meg bit her lip and nodded.

'I. . .I told you. Eve and I are just tourists, passing through the district. This isn't our dog. It's late. We haven't found anywhere to stay tonight yet and. . .'

'And you don't want any further involvement.'

There was a hint of steel in the vet's words. The good humour faded and Meg flushed. This man had echoed her wishes exactly, but she knew what he was feeling. Meg felt exactly the same when parents dumped ill children into Casualty and then, with their eyes on their wrist-watches and their feet already walking to the door, asked what time to collect them.

It wasn't the same situation. This was a stray dog, for heaven's sake.

'But. . . Look, we can't stay any longer,' she said desperately. 'We can't get any more involved than we already are. We're English tourists. The dog. . .the dog seems to be a stray. He just ran out in front of the car and. . . Please, we can't stop. Will you look after him?'

'But if we don't stay he'll put him down,' Eve said flatly from where she'd stayed, unmoving, on the passenger seat. Her hands came up to cradle the dog against her and the little dog gave a whimper of pain at the movement. Immediately the child's eyes filled with more tears. 'Oh, I've hurt him. I've hurt him again.'

She looked pleadingly up at her cousin. 'Meg, he's such a little dog. And you heard what the farmer told us when he stopped to help.' Her voice trailed off to a frightened whisper as she turned to look up to Rob Daniels.

'The farmer said he's a stray and he wanted to shoot him. And vets don't keep dogs. You don't, do you? I mean. . .' She looked uncertainly across at Rob and then out at the three magnificent collies. 'You don't operate and save them when you don't know who their owners are. I know you don't.' Her appeal gave way to a tearful glare.

'No,' Rob said gently, stooping again beside child and dog. The steel in his voice had disappeared in the face of Eve's distress. 'But I will care for him, Eve.' He placed a hand under the dog's muzzle and lifted the little head carefully—almost as if speaking to the dog himself. 'I won't let him stay in pain. I'll keep him comfortable while I make enquiries as to who owns him.'

'And if you can't find anyone?' Eve's small chin tilted, her eyes huge.

'Then, if he won't recover without an expensive operation and lots of care afterwards, I'll have to put him down,' Rob said honestly. 'I can't do more than that, Eve. You can see as well as I can that he's starving. I have a list inside of missing dogs and maybe he's on that list—but if he's not, well, if I kept every stray I find I'd have a hundred dogs. You're old enough to realise that sometimes it's kinder to put an injured dog down.'

Meg let her breath out in a rush. This man wasn't condemning her out of hand, it seemed. He wouldn't make Eve hate her for being cold-hearted. Rob Daniel's voice was kind but firm. Surely Eve would see. . .

Eve didn't. The child looked from Rob to Meg—and then back to Rob.

'He's not a stray,' she said with a voice that was tremulous. 'He's mine.'

'Eve. . .'

'He is.' Eve turned back to her cousin. 'He is, Meg. I haven't wanted anything. Not anything. Since Mum and Dad died everyone's said they'll buy me things or let me do things or they'll take me on expensive holidays, and I didn't want it. I didn't want anything, but I do now. I want this dog. This dog's like me, Meg. He hasn't got anyone. He's only got me.' Her voice trailed off into helplessness—a helplessness far more appealing than any words.

'Eve. . .' Meg's voice caught in her throat. She looked down at the still form of the dog cradled in her young cousin's arms and her heart lurched within her. 'Eve, we can't possibly keep him. Even if he lives. . .'

'Why not?' Eve whispered.

'Because we live in England, for one thing,' Meg managed. 'We'd never be able to take him home.'

'There's quarantine,' Eve said stubbornly. 'And if that takes too long then I'll just have to stay here. I might as well stay in Australia. You could go home and leave me here.'

'Eve, you know I can't. . .'

'Meg, if I keep him I'll have to eat, won't I?' Eve demanded suddenly, her huge eyes fixed on her older cousin's face. 'I'll have to eat to be well to look after him. I will, Meg. At least. . .' Her voice faltered with a trace of the self-doubt and honesty inherent in her nature. 'At least, I'll try.'

'Oh, Eve. . .' It was all Meg could do not to stoop down and hug child and dog to her. To tell Eve that of course she could keep the dog. Paralysed or not. Dying or not. Beside her, the vet was watching both girls with eyes that showed an almost detached interest. He was keeping right out of a discussion that was clearly hugely important on all levels.

'Eve, we just can't,' Meg whispered, casting the vet a look of appeal. The look was met with bland indifference. She was being left to fight her own battles here.

'We can.'

Meg looked down helplessly at the dog—and then back to the vet. His green eyes rested on her with lazy interest.

'I. . .'

'Yes?' A polite enquiry, nothing more.

He'd have to give her some help here, Meg thought savagely. He must. Meg took a deep breath, fighting for reason. Maybe. . .maybe there was quarantine. . . Maybe. . .

'I think the quarantine's three months,' the vet told her, and there was a tiny trace of laughter back behind his eyes. 'Maybe longer. I'd have to check. It's an expensive proposition, but possible. Look, may I suggest we get the dog into the surgery now and make decisions after I've seen what the damage is?'

Meg grasped the straw.

'Yes,' she said firmly. 'If you take him. . .see what has to be done. . .I'll take Eve into town and telephone after we've found a hotel.'

'No,' Eve said fiercely. She was climbing from the car but as Rob made to lift the dog from her she swerved away. 'I'll bring him in and I'm staying here while you examine him. I know exactly what you'll do if I go. You'll put him down and then Meg will say it was the only thing to do. If I see the X-ray and his back's broken then. . .then you can put him down, but otherwise. . .otherwise he's mine.'

'Eve, you can't. . .'

'Yes, I can,' Eve said fiercely, her white face grim and set. 'I'm all he's got. He's all I've got, too, and we're staying together.'

The dog's back wasn't broken.

X-rays revealed a badly fractured hind leg but little internal damage at all.

'He's been very, very lucky,' the vet said thoughtfully. He'd made them stay in the waiting-room while he set up a drip, did a complete examination and studied the X-rays. Half an hour later he came back out to them, smiling in reassurance as both girls rose to their feet.

Rob Daniels was now wearing a long white coat over his jeans—more to protect the injured dog against his horsiness than to protect his clothes, Meg thought. His white coat gave him at last an air of medical professional-ism, though it didn't detract one bit from the way Meg reacted to those hypnotic eyes. The shock of red-brown hair and the lean moulding of his face was charismatic enough—without the depths of those eyes throwing her right off balance and keeping her there.

'OK.' With difficulty Meg fought off the impact this charismatic vet was having on her. She closed her eyes wearily. This had been a long day and she'd had more than enough. 'That's. . .that's great. Is he moving again?'

'Not yet,' Rob told her. 'And I don't want him to. I've sedated him now. I'll ring my vet nurse and as soon as she comes over I'll anaesthetise him completely and set the leg. If you agree to the operation. . .'

'You mean, if we'll pay,' Meg said bluntly and the vet nodded.

'Yes.' Then, watching Meg's cold face, the man shook his head. 'Look, ma'am, if you don't want to pay to fix his leg then you don't want the dog very much. It'd be kinder to put him down now. Make a decision but make it fast.'

'We'll pay,' Eve whispered, flashing a defiant glance at Meg. 'Even if I have to pay out of my allowance. If. . .' She cast Meg another glance, this time doubtful, and turned again back to Rob. 'If you'll agree to let me pay in bits.'

Silence. Meg swallowed and swallowed again. She was so unaccustomed to her young cousin saying anything—and here was Eve hurling defiance and pleading for a dog she hardly knew.

'Paying by instalment is fine by me, Eve,' Rob Daniels told Eve gently, his eyes also resting on Meg, and Meg flushed crimson with embarrassment. She was now feeling like a particularly nasty form of tightwad.

'Oh, for heaven's sake. . . Of course I'll pay. . .'

'Will you, Meg?' Eve breathed. The child's smile was worth any money she might have to pay, Meg thought, but then Eve threw another surprise at her. Her young cousin was thinking fast. 'But Meg. . . Meg, you could do the anaesthetic. Would that make it cheaper?' The child turned back to Rob. 'Meg could help you operate because we're staying here till we can take him with us.'

'Meg. . .' The vet turned to Meg in astonishment, his eyes, perusing Meg's slim form with an assessing look that made her blush deepen. 'Are you a vet nurse, then, Meg?'

'Meg's a doctor,' Eve told him. 'Human.' Her tone told them that she thought animal doctors were far superior.

'A doctor. . .' Rob Daniels' eyes widened and his look grew thoughtful. He dug his hands deep into the pockets of his white coat and considered, his gaze not leaving Meg's face. 'Well, well. You've done some anaesthetics?'

'Yes, but. . .'

'It would help if you could give the anaesthetic,' the vet said slowly. 'My vet nurse is a mum with three kids and I hate disturbing her on a Saturday afternoon. If you could help. . . If I talked you through this. . .'

'But. . .'

'It's easy,' Rob assured her. 'I normally give anaesthetic and set a dog's leg myself, using an intravenous anaesthetic. It's only when an animal's as weak as this that I need intubation and another pair of eyes. I would appreciate it. Otherwise I'll have to disturb Sue or leave the leg until Monday, and with the amount of gravel embedded in the flesh I want it thoroughly cleaned soon.'

'But we have to get into town,' Meg said helplessly. 'We don't have time. . .'

Her voice broke off. Both the vet and her young cousin were watching Meg now as if she were deliberately providing obstacles. She was starting to feel like the big bad witch of the west, and she wasn't enjoying the sensation one bit. She was almost wishing she hadn't gone near her young cousin two months ago.

Maybe not. If she hadn't interfered Eve would be dead by now and she knew it.

'Eve, now we've agreed to the operation surely we can leave him,' Meg struggled to say. 'You must see we can't take the dog with us tonight. He's going to need constant observation—and, besides, I'll bet there's not a hotel in town that takes dogs.' She turned back to the vet. 'Is there?' she demanded.

'There's not.' The vet's expression was thoughtful as he watched Meg's face. 'But. . .'

'But what?' Meg felt driven against the ropes. Her hazel eyes flashed with frustration and she pushed a weary hand up to brush her dusty curls back from her face. Rob Daniels noted the gesture and understood.

'You're exhausted,' he said gently.

'I'm not. It's just. . .'

'That you don't know what to do. May I make a suggestion? If you like, you could stay here tonight.'

'Here?'

'Yes. Here.'

Meg stared. She took a deep breath and shook her head in bewilderment. 'No. I. . .'

'Meg, listen to what he says,' Eve interjected suddenly. 'You must. It's just plain mean not to listen when he's being so nice to us.'

So nice. . .

Meg flashed a look up to the vet—a look that told him that 'nice' wasn't the first adjective that sprang to her tongue—and to her disgust, laughter swept back over Rob Daniels' face.

'Have you ever noted how bossy and overbearing human doctors are?' Rob asked Eve, his laughter encompassing both of them. 'Making decisions out of hand! Animal doctors are never like that. Animal doctors are meek, tolerant and totally reasonable human beings.'

'I'll bet they are,' Meg muttered, refusing to meet those laughter-filled eyes.

'Now here we have three people,' Rob continued,

speaking only to Eve. 'Two of us are totally reasonable. Eve, you've found yourself a nice Australian dog to take home as a souvenir and a lifetime companion, and I'd like to patch him up so he'll be a credit to his country. And here I am offering you the best accommodation this side of paradise and you, an obviously agreeable young lady, wish at least to listen to my offer. It's only this lady doctor here refusing to listen. Do they teach crabbiness at medical school, do you think?'

Meg glared. She couldn't speak. She couldn't think of a single thing to say.

'Will you agree to at least listen?' the vet asked Meg with mock servility, and Meg's glare deepened. So did Rob Daniels's laughter as he turned once again to Eve.

'I have a huge farmhouse,' he told Eve, with only a sideways glance at her enraged cousin. 'This place belonged to my parents, and my grandparents before them, and it has five bedrooms, for heaven's sake! I have a number of indigent friends and relatives who treat this place as a free holiday house so the beds are always made up, but just at the moment I'm relative-free. So. . .I'm offering free board and lodging in return for your Dr Meg helping me fix up your four-legged mate. What could be more reasonable than that?'

'And you'll charge like a wounded bull for the operation, I'll bet,' Meg snapped.

And then she flushed all over again. Whoa. . .

She caught herself. What a totally horrid thing to say when this man was being. . . How had Eve described him? Nice? It seemed that Rob Daniels was nice. It was a truly kind offer. So why on earth had it thrown Meg into such confusion?

It was just the way Rob Daniels looked at her. All he had to do was smile and Meg was thrown right off balance.

'I. . .I'm sorry. . .' she stammered. 'I didn't mean to be rude. . .'

'So I should hope.' Rob Daniels's voice sounded wounded to the core—but when Meg ventured to look up into his face she saw nothing but that constant, lurking laughter. Laughter so infectious that, despite weariness, confusion and misgivings, Meg wanted to smile right back.

And finally that lurking laughter was just too much and she did.

Meg's tired face lit with the sense of the ridiculous that was almost second nature to her before she'd had to cope with Eve.

'Of. . .of course I'll help with the dog,' she managed unsteadily. 'I am sorry. Just show me what to do. But. . . But Eve and I can't trespass on your hospitality. We don't even. . .'

Rob's look had grown intent. He'd watched Meg's face transform into laughter with fascination, as though somehow he found Meg's commonplace hazel eyes just as hypnotic as Meg found his green ones.

'You don't even know me?' Rob finished for her in that deep, rich voice that resonated round the room and drew Meg's attention to him like a magnet. His eyes grew suddenly grave. 'Neither you do. I could be up to all sorts of villainy, offering you a bed for the night.

'But, if you think about it, I am the local vet and I do have my reputation to consider. If I filled my backyard with skeletons of damsels in distress the vet board might take away my licence and I'd be all upset. But you, on the other hand. . .' His eyes travelled thoughtfully from Meg to Eve and back to Meg again as his laughter deepened.

'On the other hand, you two might be villains. How do I know you haven't left a string of country vets murdered in your wake? Or maybe. . .' his voice grew low with foreboding '. . .maybe you chop them up and stuff them in your suitcases to take home as souvenirs. Maybe I should inspect all baggage before I agree to offer hospitality.'

Beside Meg, Eve giggled.

And, as Meg's humour bubbled up again, she was lost. Meg looked down into Eve's face and saw the child's face creased into lines of laughter—and she knew that a miracle was happening here.

Eve hadn't smiled in months. The child hadn't even looked like smiling. And here she was, giggling like. . .like the thirteen-year-old she really was.

Well, Meg had travelled halfway round the world searching for that laughter; searching for the child she was starting to believe was lost for ever—and she'd found the child here.

Good grief!

Somehow Meg was landing herself with an injured dog and the hospitality of a vet she didn't trust one inch—even though murder and mayhem weren't the things she suspected him of. Despite all the problems, though, Eve's laughter was compelling. Meg spread her hands—and gave in against overwhelming odds.

'If you look in our baggage all you'll find is dirty washing and a few souvenir koalas. Not one chopped-up vet, I promise.' She smiled uncertainly. 'Thank. . .thank you. It seems we'd love to accept your offer. Wouldn't we, Eve?'

'Yes, please,' Eve breathed and the magic smile stayed with her.

'Right.'

The laughter was fading from Rob Daniels' face even as Meg spoke. It was as if he'd achieved what he'd been working for and was now intent on the next step. 'That's it, then. Baggage-searching can wait. We have one very sick dog to attend to, Dr. . . Dr. . .'

'Dr Preston,' Meg told him. 'I'm Meg Preston and this is my cousin, Eve McKay.'

'I'm pleased to meet you, Dr Meg Preston and Miss Eve McKay,' Rob said briefly. 'But we don't have time for more social chat. I've had saline up and it's already going through. Your dog seems badly dehydrated as well as starving, so I want to put fluid on board before operating. Now, though. . .'

'Now you want to operate?' Eve asked.

Rob gave the child a reassuring smile. 'We must,' he agreed. 'The sooner the better. There's so much gravel in the wound that the gravel itself is impeding circulation. And this could take a while, Eve,' he warned. 'Don't think the worst if we're not out of Theatre for an hour or so.

'While you're waiting I suggest you take the dogs, find the hens who are out somewhere near the sheds and then instigate an egg hunt. I've bacon in the fridge and plenty of bread, but if we want eggs and bacon for tea it's up to you, Eve, to find our dinner. If anything really urgent happens—some farmer comes looking for me and it's a bigger problem than we have here—then ring the front doorbell and if I can I'll come out. Now let's move.'

Eve stared.

And then, to Meg's utter astonishment, Eve gave a snappy girl-guide salute, giggled once more, turned on her heel and disappeared hen-wards.

Meg practically gaped. This was her non-responsive cousin?

'And now us,' Rob said, his expression growing more serious. He took Meg's arm and looked thoughtfully down at her face. 'You are overtired,' he said softly. 'Are you sure you can cope?'

On top of all this, sympathy. It was too much.

'I. . .I can cope,' Meg said with quiet dignity—but a part of her was answering in another way as he led her through to the surgery at the back of the house.

I'm just not sure I can cope with you, Rob Daniels, was her silent rejoinder. I'm not sure in the least.

CHAPTER THREE

IT TOOK time, patience and skill to repair the damage to the little dog.

Rob Daniels showed patience and skill in abundance. He also showed trust.

Swiftly Rob outlined what he needed Meg to do, assuming professional competency as a matter of course. Meg appreciated the compliment. She was an unknown overseas doctor. Would she have been as trusting of some newcomer in her sphere of work?

Trusting. . .

That's what was so different about Rob Daniels. It seemed that he'd summed Meg up, found her acceptable and was acting accordingly.

Would Paul have been as generous?

Impossible comparison! Paul was a highly competent neurosurgeon. His practice in the heart of London was now so busy that he could select the work he wanted and he could select the people he wished to help him. Paul suffered no one, not even students, to encroach on his territory. Not even to watch him operate. . .

Meg shook the thought of Paul away. It was strange how little she had thought of him over the past weeks. She gave herself a guilty mental shake and focussed her attention totally on the job at hand.

Thankfully, anaesthetising dogs wasn't all that different from anaesthetising humans.

'He must have been close to death before you hit him,' Rob murmured as he cleared torn fur from injured flesh. They'd scrubbed swiftly. Rob had outlined what he needed and now he left Meg to her work as he concen-

trated on his. 'It's my guess that's why he's not trying
to move. The shock and pain, on top of general debilitation, were just too much for him. He's decided to lie
down and die.'

Like Eve had, Meg thought grimly, attending fiercely
to her equipment.

It was suddenly intensely important that this little dog
lived. There were so many difficulties facing Meg in
getting this small creature healthy and back to London—
but the difficulties seemed almost minor compared to
Eve's reaction if the dog died.

Meg hardly spoke as she worked, and Rob respected
her need for concentration. He gave clear, precise instructions as he worked on the damaged leg, his eyes checking
Meg's movements every few moments with an
expression that gave her assurance. She was on her own,
yet not. . .

The bone was completely shattered at the break and
it was a lengthy and tedious job to remove the gravel
and the splinters of bone from the damaged flesh. The
bone itself was too badly broken for simple external
fixation. It had to be fixed internally, and inserting a
medullary nail and fusing bone and nail into something
that would give the limb strength and mobility was a
long and tedious task.

The fracture was oblique so that Rob was forced to
add encircling wires for additional stability. It was the
same process as used in humans, Meg noted, realising
with shock that in human operations of this sort the bone
was usually much larger. Rob Daniels's job here was, in
fact, more complicated—as complex as the work of a
skilled paediatric surgeon, working on infants.

'It'd be easier to amputate,' Meg murmured and Rob
nodded, his eyes not leaving his work.

'Yes,' Rob answered briefly. 'But, with luck, now he'll
have a working leg, even if it is stiff. If you and your

cousin don't end up taking him back to England he has a better chance of finding a home if he's not obviously disfigured.'

'We will take him,' Meg said firmly—but Rob shot her a look that said he wasn't too sure whether to believe her.

Finally Rob closed the major wound, manipulating flesh over rebuilt bone with care as he checked and rechecked damaged nerves and blood vessels.

Finally he turned his attention to debriding the dog's injured hindquarters. The car had obviously propelled the little dog hard into gravel, and it was a long and painstaking task to clear the debris embedded in the wasted flesh.

'Even when his leg heals he won't be a respectable pup for a long, long time,' Rob told Meg as he eventually completed the cleansing. He dressed the wound with care and adjusted intravenous antibiotics through the drip. The drip had been already running when Meg came into Theatre—the saline had been given as a measure against shock, as well as to rehydrate, and the drip would now provide nutrition as well as prevent infection. 'I don't think your cousin's going to have a cute pup. . .'

'I know,' Meg whispered, 'but I don't think a cute pup is what my cousin needs.'

Rob cast Meg a curious look as he moved to take over the anaesthetic. Meg stepped back to let him reverse. Now she was no longer needed it was sensible for Rob to perform something he was much more skilled at than Meg. Still she watched those skilled hands. . .surgeon's hands. . .

In London this man could make a fortune, Meg thought suddenly. With Rob Daniels' charm and skills he could demand huge fees as a small-animal doctor.

Paul had gone for the big money when choosing his profession. Why not this man?

There was that comparison again. Paul and Rob Daniels. . . Alike in some ways—in their surgical skill, for instance—but in others as different as chalk and cheese.

Meg stood silent, her mind working slowly over the comparison as Rob moved the small dog over to a heated pad in a cage at the edge of the room. He shifted the drip paraphernalia with him and Meg marvelled at the man's dexterity.

'You're used to orderlies and nurses to shift your patients,' Rob smiled, waving away Meg's offers to help. He settled the little dog and gave him a brief rub behind the ears. 'There you go, mate. You'll do. You just sleep off the anaesthetic and concentrate on getting better.' Then he turned back to Meg.

'Us animal doctors get to lug our own patients round,' he smiled. 'It gets a bit harder than this when I'm treating Hereford bulls—or Clydesdale horses.'

'I'll bet.' Meg crossed to the sink and they peeled off gloves together and started to wash. 'Do you have many Clydesdales to practise on?' she asked curiously.

'Not as many as I'd like,' Rob told her. 'They're lovely horses. Souls like true gentlemen. I'd much rather treat a Clydesdale than a nasty little Shetland pony. I've a few ponies in my practice that make pit bull terriers and Dobermanns look like pussies in comparison.'

Meg smiled absently, elbow-deep in suds. She looked over at their patient, still solidly sleeping off the effects of the trauma. 'Will. . .will he be. . .?'

'I don't see why he shouldn't recover,' Rob told her, following the direction of her gaze. 'The X-rays showed little sign of internal damage. The lungs are sound and his breathing's steady. All he has to cope with now is shock and general debilitation. It'll be a long road to recovery, though—with some difficult decisions along the way.'

'Meaning?'

'Meaning, despite your promises, are you really going to keep him?'

Meg fell silent. She'd donned a green theatre gown over her bloodstained clothes, and Rob moved behind her to untie it. The feel of his hands at her waist was strangely unnerving. Such a simple procedure done a thousand times during Meg's medical career—yet when Rob performed it. . .

When he touched her she once again had that feeling that here was a man who could lift the cares from her shoulders. . .

That was nonsense. She gave herself an angry shrug and turned to face him.

Then she wished she hadn't. Rob Daniels was too close for comfort. Very much too close—with those caring, concerned eyes. . .

'Yes. We'll keep him,' she managed, 'if he lives. . .' Her voice sounded breathless, as though she'd run a mile—or was making some superhuman effort. . .

'May I ask why?' Rob's look was intent. He stood staring down at the tired girl before him as though trying to make her out.

'You heard. Eve wants. . .'

'And what Eve wants Eve gets?'

'If it'll make a difference.'

'I see.' The piercing green eyes looked down at Meg and Meg knew that he did see. It didn't need his quiet words to confirm that he'd summed Eve up and come to the right conclusion. 'Anorexia nervosa?'

'Yes.' Meg shrugged. 'It's obvious, isn't it?'

'Well, she's obviously severely malnourished. Your cousin must weigh half the weight she should.'

Meg thought back to Eve's matchstick arms and legs, and the shrunken eyes in her too-pale face and she nodded. Meg couldn't expect people not to notice. She just had to be grateful that this man had made no comment to Eve herself.

'She looks like she should be in hospital,' Rob said gently. 'Instead of traipsing round strange countries.'

'I took her out of hospital,' Meg told him, her voice betraying an inner weariness which was almost overwhelming. 'Two months ago. She'd just recovered from a bout of pneumonia and the pneumonia had nearly killed her. The hospital staff were feeding her intravenously, but Eve was fighting them every inch of the way. All she wanted to do was to die, and she came very close.'

'And. . . Is there a reason why she's starving herself?' Rob was frowning in concentration, his thoughts obviously with the waif-like child waiting for them outside. 'She seems a nice kid. Is there any background problem?'

'Just. . .overwhelming loneliness and guilt,' Meg told him slowly. There was a part of Meg that was wondering just why on earth she was talking to this man—but another part of her that welcomed the chance. She'd carried this burden by herself for too long.

'My cousin's an only child of cold-hearted parents who hadn't really wanted her. When she was twelve they shunted her off to boarding school. She hated it but they wouldn't let her come home. Eve ran away. . .many times, I gather. The last time. . . The last time she ran away at night and the school asked her parents to come down because she was missing.

'It was midwinter, my uncle's car skidded on snow and my aunt and uncle were killed. Eve. . . Well, they tell me Eve was close to anorexic before then but afterwards she just refused point-blank to eat anything. She was very close to death before I found her.'

'You found her. . .'

'Well, her headmistress found me.' Meg shrugged. She started folding her theatre gown into meticulous creases, as if it was to be put away for a fussy owner rather than be laundered. 'It sounds dreadful, doesn't it, but when her headmistress found me I hardly knew I had a cousin?' She looked up at Rob, willing him to understand. This was important.

'My mother and Eve's mother were sisters but. . .my mother was a single mum and Aunt Olive never came near us. Mum knew Olive and her husband had a daughter, but Eve and I had nothing to do with each other as cousins. I didn't know my aunt and uncle were dead— that's how far apart our families were. It was only when Eve grew so ill that her headmistress set her own enquiries in place, searching desperately for any sort of family.'

'So you walked straight into a nightmare,' Rob said slowly.

'Not at first,' Meg told him honestly. 'My. . .my mum had been very bitter about her family. Mum died of cancer five years ago and I'd contacted Aunt Olive then—asking her to see Mum before she died. My aunt refused—called me an illegitimate brat and said that Mum and I were no part of her family.

'Even after she was dead it was hard to feel as if Olive's family had any hold on me. But then. . .well, Eve was only thirteen. I kept telling myself that she was Olive's daughter but the bottom line was that she was still my cousin and I also had no family. So I went to see her. And found her. . .'

'Dying?'

'Yes,' Meg confessed. 'They. . . The hospital staff had almost given up. They said that she was so psychologically damaged there was no way they could save her. The only way she'd be fed was if they kept her close to unconscious and fed her intravenously, and they couldn't keep her sedated for the rest of her life. So. . .I took leave without pay from the hospital and tried. . .tried. . .'

'Tried to save her,' Rob said slowly. 'A kid you didn't

know.' He shook his head, as if he couldn't believe what he was hearing, and the look he gave Meg was as if he were seeing her for the first time. 'But. . . Why did you come to Australia?'

'Because it was so different,' Meg told him. 'At first I took Eve home to my hospital flat, but it didn't work. She wasn't well enough to go to school and in my small flat I found us trapped inside with the food issue growing bigger and bigger. At first Eve promised she'd eat if I took her out of hospital, and if I watched her like a hawk she would eat a little. Only then she'd go to the toilet and make herself ill.

'So I thought. . .if we came on a holiday. . .went touring and kept her busy. . . If I shared hotel rooms with her and even. . .even ate and then drove for three or four hours after eating so she'd have to digest something before there was an opportunity for her to make herself ill, then maybe she'd recover. And to a certain extent it's worked. Eve's stronger now than when we left. Only when we go back. . .'

'You've achieved little,' Rob said gently. 'You know she'll revert.'

'Yes,' Meg said wearily. 'I'm not fooling myself. I haven't achieved any miracle, except in keeping her alive for a few more months.'

'While you put your own life on hold.' Rob nodded. 'And now. . .this dog? How is he going to complicate things?'

'I hope. . .I hope he won't. This dog's the first thing I've seen Eve interested in all the time I've known her,' Meg confessed. 'The first. She's been like a porcelain doll, with a fixed expression on her face that I haven't been able to change. Everything that happens Eve just reacts to with polite disinterest. There've been no tears and there's been no laughter.

'But today. . .today Eve cried because she thought the

pup was going to die. You made her giggle and she
pleaded with me to keep the dog—and it was as if
windows were being opened. Her headmistress says
there's a bright, enquiring mind in there—a dear little
girl, her headmistress calls her—but until today I'd never
really believed it. So. . . How can I refuse to take care
of the dog? How can I slam the windows shut again?'

'You can't,' Rob said bluntly. 'But where does that
leave you?'

'With a dog,' Meg smiled wearily. 'If he lives. And,
you see. . .he must live.'

'He must, indeed.' Rob looked over to where the little
dog's sides rose and fell in a steady rhythm, reassuring
both Meg and Rob with the evenness of his breathing.
The vet nodded in satisfaction. 'But if he does. . .heaven
knows what sort of a dog he is. He could turn out to
be vicious or stupid or. . . Did you say you live in a
hospital flat?'

'Yes.'

'I can't see a dog fitting in there. Can you?'

'I'll have to find somewhere else,' Meg said
doubtfully.

'And what about quarantine?' Rob said bluntly. 'It'll
be damned expensive. Did Eve's parents leave her well
provided for?'

'No,' Meg told him. She sighed. 'But I'll manage.
Somehow.'

There was a long moment of silence. Meg saw her
future yawning before her, almost as a bottomless chasm.
What now? Could Eve go back to boarding school with
a dog? She couldn't—and a part of Meg that had been
denying the future for a long time was starting to come
to the surface with overwhelming force. Even if Eve did
recover Meg couldn't send her back to school. Eve must
have a family. She must. And Meg was that family. . .

And Paul?

How would Paul react to this instant family? Paul wanted Meg, but Meg was under no illusions as to how this forsaken pup and emotionally starved child would fit into Paul's well-ordered existence. She thought of Paul's chrome and glass apartment, with its wonderful views and fussy housekeeper, and she winced.

There were some hard decisions to be made.

She couldn't make them.

One day at a time, she told herself drearily, and lifted her eyes to find Rob Daniels watching her with an expression that told her he was with her all the way.

'Let's just get our pup's drip checked and our Eve fed and bedded down for the night,' he said softly. 'Then you can sit and stare at the stars and confront all your worries. But one step at a time, Dr Preston.'

And Meg looked up at Rob Daniels' kindly, concerned face, and it was all she could do not to burst into tears.

One step at a time. . .

CHAPTER FOUR

Eve had found fourteen eggs.

Meg's young cousin was seated at the kitchen table when they emerged, her eyes so filled with anxiety that Meg winced. Eve's long blonde hair was wet around her face where it had rested against tearful cheeks.

The child's hands were clenched in front of her, and there were traces of blood on her wrists. Her fingernails had been pushed so hard into her palms that she'd made herself bleed. Under the table Rob's collies lay and watched their new young friend with obvious concern.

'So, what will you call your dog, young Eve?' Rob demanded as he ushered Meg into the kitchen. Like Meg, Rob's eyes obviously noted Eve's distress but he made no comment. 'He needs a name,' Rob continued, smiling down at the child's woebegone face. 'But I doubt anything dignified will do. If, you call a dog like this Alphonso or Bertrand people will snigger behind his back. I suggest something a bit more earthy to match his nature. How about Spud?'

Eve's hands unclenched. The wide, staring eyes shifted from Meg to Rob, and the child opened her mouth to speak. When she did her voice came out as a terrified whisper.

'He's. . .he's going to live?'

'He has a good chance of living,' Rob said gently, sitting opposite Eve at the table and taking her hands in his. 'He may well have a limp but I think we've even saved his leg. All he need now is lots and lots of TLC.'

'TLC?'

'Tender loving care.' Rob smiled. 'It'll take some work

to nurse him back to health, though, Eve, and heaps of patience.'

'I. . .I'll do it.' Eve cast a scared look up at Meg. 'But, Meg, I've. . . I've been thinking of the problems. . .I mean, how will we get him home? If he has to stay in quarantine I won't be able to look after him. Maybe I could go to boarding school here. . .a school that lets me take him. . .'

'Let's cross that bridge when we come to it,' Meg told her, stooping to give the child a swift hug. 'We'll keep this disreputable mutt with us, if you insist—Spud, is it? But whatever happens there's three of us in this. There's you, there's me and there's Spud, and if you think I'm letting my only family stay here while I go back to England you have another think coming. You and I are family now, Eve—or rather you, me and Spud—and you'll have to get used to me.'

'But you don't really want me,' Eve whispered. 'You and Paul. . .'

'We're a chain,' Meg smiled, crouching down and taking the child's hands in hers as Rob released them. Rob was watching silently, his face concerned. 'You love Spud, Eve. I love you, and back in England Paul loves me. That sounds like a family to me.'

It didn't at all, Meg admitted to herself. It sounded like an absolute disaster but there was no doubt sounding in Meg's voice. She still held the child's hands, and her grip tightened. 'What do you think of Spud for a name?'

Eve's face lightened a little, and to Meg's delight a smile flittered into her eyes. She looked across at Rob. 'Spud. . .I like it but. . . If spuds are potatoes then he's not really fat enough to be a Spud.'

'He's dirty enough,' Rob said promptly. 'And as for fat, well, that's up to you, young lady. If you're as soft a touch as your cousin here I reckon your dog will be waddling within six months. And, speaking of food. . .'

He looked approvingly into the basket of eggs on the table. 'Well done, Eve. I haven't found an egg for a week.'

'I found them in the bushes out behind the sheds,' Eve told him. 'The hens must hide them really well. I think there's more there but. . .I got a bit anxious and came inside to wait.'

'I can understand that,' Rob smiled. He crossed to the fridge, hauled it open and tossed Eve a loaf of bread. 'You can continue your egg-hunting tomorrow. OK, Eve. I'm heading for a fast shower and then I'll fry the bacon. Meg's on egg duty after she's degrimed—I'll have three, please, Dr Preston, and I like them sunny side up. And you're on toast duty, young Eve. Let's get cooking.'

It was the first meal Meg had enjoyed for two long months.

Meals with Eve had been a nightmare, with Eve forcing down every mouthful and trying every way she knew to avoid eating. Now. . . Now Rob had her laughing so much that she hardly noticed she was eating.

And Eve did eat. Not much. Meg wasn't asking for miracles here and, indeed, if Eve had eaten a normal-sized meal her stomach would probably have rejected it—but she managed toast, bacon and most of her egg. No comment was passed on how much she was eating. Rob Daniels had sense as well as kindness, Meg decided, and the mood was totally relaxed. Afterwards Rob brought coffee out to the verandah and then, as Eve demurred on coffee, he disappeared inside again and emerged with a glass of milk.

'Strawberry milk,' he pronounced, and Eve lifted the glass and stared at it in confusion. The milk was creamy white.

'Strawberry. . .?'

'From my very own cow, Strawberry,' Rob smiled. 'You'll meet her in the morning. Taste her milk and see

if it isn't the best you've ever tried in your young life.'
And then he started talking to Meg, as if he didn't mind
whether Eve drank or not.

And Eve sipped and sipped again—and Meg noted
the child's fingers coming out to the side table and taking
one or two of the grapes from the bowl Rob had placed
within reach. A miracle indeed!

And Meg finally found herself relaxing. Rob was telling them about his cow—a very silly anecdote about
Strawberry's follies as a calf—and Meg found her tension slipping away as he spoke. Her instincts were right
about this man. Here was someone who could lift Meg's
cares from her shoulders—at least for a day or two.

Soon they'd come crashing back, but for
tonight. . .tonight Meg could sit under the stars and let
Rob entertain her with his nonsense stories, invented to
make Eve laugh, and she could feel nothing but overwhelming gratitude.

She didn't want to move. She'd been on holiday for
two months now and this was the first night she felt in
a holiday mood.

Rob's dogs had chosen a human apiece and lay bliss-
fully at their feet, comforting with their undemanding
presence. Meg looked out at the stars emerging in the
night sky over the sea. She listened to the surf crash on
the beach below the house and Meg felt overwhelming
peace. Rob had told her that she could confront her
worries while watching the stars, but who could see
worries in stars like these? Their brilliance was incred-
ible. In London Meg so rarely saw stars. This was like
another world.

'I think your cousin's going to sleep,' Rob told Eve,
and Meg turned to find both watching her, the smile
she delighted in seeing still playing on Eve's lips. Meg
flushed.

'I was just thinking. . .'

'Of Paul?' Eve asked bluntly. The child's face clouded momentarily but then the smile returned and she flashed Meg a look of mischief.

'Who's Paul?' Rob queried.

'Paul's Meg's fiancé,' Eve told him. 'He's the biggest stuffed shirt in London but Meg thinks he's cute.' She cast Meg a look of defiance. 'It shows how blind love can be.'

'Well, you've fallen in love at first sight with the most misbegotten mongrel known to mankind,' Meg retorted, returning her cousin's defiance with a grin, but the euphoria faded. She looked doubtfully at Eve. 'I. . . Eve, if Dr Daniels shows us where to sleep then maybe we'd better get you to bed. . .'

'I was just thinking the same thing myself,' Rob said gravely. He rose. 'But first maybe Eve would like to check her pup. I've been checking every time I go inside and last time he was stirring. I think it'd be best if it was Eve he grew accustomed to as he woke up.'

'Oh, yes. . .' Eve was on her feet in a moment. She cast a doubtful look at Meg. 'Because I'll be his owner for ever. . .'

It took a while to tear Eve from her recovering pup. The dog was still limp and half-asleep, but when Eve stroked the sad little face his ragged tail lifted a fraction from the mat and gave the feeblest of wags.

It was enough. 'See. He knows me. He's my friend already,' Eve whispered. The child fondled the little face, and Meg bit back a comment about fleas and infections as a pink tongue come out and licked Eve's cheek. Sometimes there were more important considerations than the odd germ.

'I can take him to sleep on my bed if I'm really careful with the tubes,' Eve tried, but Rob smiled and shook his head.

'I need to check on him through the night, young lady, and your bed is hardly a hospital ward. He needs a firm, warm bed, he needs the equipment that's in my surgery and he therefore needs to stay right here. Say goodnight and see your friend in the morning, Eve.'

And Eve grimaced—but then smiled and went bedwards with a lighter step than Meg had ever seen the child use.

Rob showed them through to two adjoining rooms at the back of the house. He swung open the first door and Meg stopped dead in surprise.

'Oh, for heaven's sake! We can't stay here,' she said, taken aback. The bathroom Rob had showed her to before dinner was grand enough, but this. . .

'Why not?' Rob demanded, with his mock-wounded air. 'Aren't my guest rooms up to standard?'

They were certainly up to standard—wide gracious rooms with a double bed apiece, magnificent polished floors, rich rugs and curtains and wide French windows, looking out to the verandah beyond.

'These. . .these are your guest rooms?' Eve gasped, and Rob grinned.

'Nope. I kicked the butler and the second footman out to sleep in the stables tonight. They don't mind. They're used to the whims of a tyrannical master.'

Eve giggled but Meg was still looking doubtful.

'Look, we really shouldn't. . .'

'It's too late to have qualms,' Rob told her firmly. 'You're in my power until morning. So. . . If I were you I'd bolt the doors, get under the covers and stay until dawn.'

'Wh-why?' Eve giggled, and Rob gave the child a look of mock menace. He schooled his features into awful solemnity.

'Because from midnight until dawn is when the owner of this castle conducts his ghastly experiments,' he intoned awfully. 'With a test tube in my hand, lady, I'm a sight to curl your pyjamas. Now. . .make your escape while the going's good. In other words—hop it.'

Eve gave Rob a wondering glance, he took one step closer—and she hopped it. Meg was left alone in the corridor with this enigmatic, laughing vet. A vet like no man she'd ever met before.

'You're. . .you're very kind,' she began, half laughing as well. 'I don't know how. . .'

'To repay you?' Rob smiled, and his eyes perused Meg's face with care. The wonderful smile faded, to be replaced by a look of uncertainty. 'Never mind that, Dr Preston. I have all sorts of ideas in my head about repayments, and some time soon. . .some time soon I'm bound to let you know a way you can make them.' He placed a hand on her shoulder in a gesture of reassurance and his smile returned, gentle and compassionate. 'Goodnight, Meg. Don't worry about your dog or your cousin tonight. You have enough on your plate without that.'

Despite her weariness, Meg couldn't sleep. She was magnificently comfortable after months of assorted hotel beds and she was dead tired, but sleep was elusive. Meg lay wide awake in her luxurious bed and gazed at the ceiling, letting the events of the day drift through her tired mind. They were jumbled together as a kaleidoscope of impressions, the overriding one being the image of one Rob Daniels.

What sort of a man was he? Landowner? Farmer? Vet? Surely he didn't do all those jobs at once?

Rob had enough in his life to keep him busy without taking in strays like Meg and Eve and their injured dog, Meg thought, remembering his last comment. He'd said the same of her. Meg had enough on her plate. . .

She certainly had. Six months ago Meg had been a single girl without a tie. Now. . . Now she had a cousin who needed Meg as much as the child needed a mother. Meg was also now responsible for one mutt—Spud— who needed TLC as well as heaps of medical care. . .

As well as which, Meg had a fiancé.

Paul!

Meg's eyes flew wide in the darkness. She jerked up in bed like a jack-in-the-box. Whoops. . .

It was close to midnight. That meant it was late Saturday morning UK time. She'd promised to ring Paul.

There was a phone in the hallway. Meg had seen it during the evening. Surely Rob wouldn't mind. . .

She knew Rob wouldn't. Those compassionate eyes would surely be the last to hold anger.

Meg fished ten dollars from her purse. That should be enough. Ten Australian dollars were worth nearly five pounds, for heaven's sake, and she didn't want to talk to Paul for that long. Gripping the money in fingers that were far too tense, she padded along the polished boards of the passageway on her bare toes.

How would she tell Paul about the dog? Heaven alone knew—but he had to find out sooner or later, and waiting wouldn't make the telling one bit easier.

Paul was waiting for her call. Meg's fiancé answered on the first ring. His deep, measured tones sounded as clearly across half a world as if Paul were in the next room.

'Meg. I've been waiting at home for two hours now for this call. I have ward rounds to do and a meeting at lunchtime I'll be late for now.'

'I'm so sorry,' Meg told him contritely. 'I just. . . Paul, something's happened.'

'Eve's ill?'

Illness was what Paul was expecting, Meg knew. During the whole time Meg had planned this trip Paul had told her she was a fool. 'The child's heading for death anyway,' he'd said bluntly. 'All that'll happen by taking her to Australia is that she'll collapse in some hick country town and I'll have to drop everything and fly over to collect you when she dies.'

'Australia has excellent medical facilities,' Meg had protested. 'As good as ours.'

'Yes, but you're going nowhere I can pull strings.'

Paul's string-pulling hadn't helped Eve up to now, Meg had decided, and had flown to Australia against Paul's advice. Paul was still angry.

'No, Eve's not ill,' Meg told him now, an edge of defensiveness in her voice. 'But we hit a dog with the car this afternoon and we've spent time. . . Well, we're still at the vet's now.'

'At the vet's!' There was an incredulous intake of breath as Paul did some rough calculations. 'Meg, it must be midnight your time.'

'I know,' Meg said with a sigh. 'We're sleeping here.'

'You're sleeping in a vet's surgery?'

'Oh, for heaven's sake, Paul. . .' Meg flushed. She stared down at her bare toes and sought for an explanation that would pacify Paul and seem as reasonable as Rob's offer of accommodation really was. 'It's just. . . We're in the middle of nowhere, Paul. The vet offered to put us up and Eve. . . Eve was so upset I thought we should stay.'

'Eve's upset.' Paul latched on to this tangible piece of information and held on. 'She's upset about the dog.'

'Yes.'

'Is the dog dead?' Paul asked in a voice filled with foreboding.

'Well, no. . .'

'Do you know who the owner is?'

'He's a stray. But, Paul. . .'

'No!' Paul's blast down the phone made Meg wince. 'No, Meg. Do you hear? That kid has you running round in circles. She twists you round her little finger and you don't see. For God's sake, Meg, you can't look after a dog. Next thing she'll be wanting to bring it back to England—and I'll just bet it's not a purebred either. Is it?'

Meg thought briefly of Spud's dubious ancestry and, despite her distress, a small smile played at the corner of her lips.

'Let's just say a lot's gone into his breeding,' she managed.

Paul didn't laugh. 'Meg. . .' There was a moment's pregnant silence and when Paul spoke again his voice was back to that of measured calm, as befitted eminent surgeon pronouncing sentence on patient.

'Meg, there is no way I'll have a mongrel in this apartment,' he stated flatly. 'And you'll find there will be no boarding schools willing to accommodate the damned thing if Eve's ever fit to return to school. No matter how hysterical the child becomes, get rid of the dog and get out of there fast. Do you hear?'

'But. . .'

'I don't want buts on this, Meg,' Paul said flatly. 'I'm late for my ward round already. I love you, sweetheart, but you must be sensible. Ring me tomorrow when you're rid of the dog.'

And the phone went dead.

Silence.

'You must be sensible. . .' That was just like Paul. Well, that was why Meg had agreed to marry Paul in the first place, she thought grimly. Because they were both sensible people.

Meg carefully replaced the receiver and stared down at her pale bare toes in the moonlight. She took a deep breath, sighed—and turned to find Rob Daniels watching her from the shadows.

She jumped about a foot.

'R-Rob.'

Rob smiled, his face just discernible in the dim light but kindness was still apparent there for all that.

'I didn't mean to scare you,' he said gently. 'Don't faint. I promise I'm not a ghost.'

'You certainly move like one,' Meg said with more sharpness than she'd intended and then flushed. 'I'm sorry. I didn't even ask if. . .if I could use your phone.'

'Of course you can.' Rob crossed to where Meg's ten dollars lay in a shaft of moonlight on the hall table. He lifted it and looked quizzically down at Meg. 'I don't think you talked long enough to justify ten dollars—even if it was to England.'

'I. . .' Meg shrugged. 'It was to England but if it's too much put it toward. . .toward Spud's bill.'

Rob placed the money back on the table, folded his arms and surveyed Meg with care. He was fully dressed, Meg noted self-consciously, though not in the same clothes he'd worn at dinner. He was now in grubby jeans and a stained work shirt with some sort of canvas apron wrapped around his front.

Meg felt at a huge disadvantage in her flimsy nightie and bare feet. Her curls wisped down over her bare shoulders and she shook them forward over her breasts, as if the gesture could somehow make her a little more respectable.

'Was that the fiancé?' Rob asked softly, his eyes searching her face, and Meg nodded.

'Yes. But I. . .I'm sorry. I should have asked.'

'There's no need to be sorry. But. . .' Rob flicked on the table lamp and looked more closely at her, noting the lines of strain round Meg's eyes. 'I gather your Paul didn't take kindly to the coming of Spud into your lives.'

'No,' Meg said miserably. 'He didn't.'

'And now you don't know what to do.'

'It's not that.' Meg took a deep breath. 'We're keeping Spud. Paul will get used to the idea.'

'Do you think he will?'

'I don't know,' Meg whispered. Then she shrugged. 'I'm sorry. This isn't your concern. If you keep Spud alive for us then we can't ask any more from you.'

'I'll keep Spud alive. I've just been in to check. Spud wagged his tail again when he saw me arrive—a feeble wag, to be sure, but still a wag for all that. He's no longer dehydrated. The nourishment going through the drip is doing its job and I suspect he's a nice little dog under-neath the battering.'

'Is that why you're still awake?' Meg asked curiously. 'Because you're checking on your animals?' She looked dubiously down at his grubby jeans and strange apron.

Rob grinned. 'I don't dress to check my small animals,' he smiled. 'I've never had a patient faint yet for seeing me in my pyjamas—in fact, my dogs and cats seem to quite like them, spots and all. But I haven't been to bed yet. I've changed in preparation for an event of major significance and now I'm waiting for a miracle.'

'A miracle?'

Rob's smile deepened. 'Would you like to see my miracle?' He looked down at Meg's bare toes, pale against the floorboards in the lamplight. 'In fact, I'd appreciate your help, if you're willing. I'd like to record my miracle on video and I need a cameraman. Or camerawoman. If I give you thirty seconds to find a wrap and something to put on your feet then I promise you a miracle, Meg Preston, as long as you're capable of hold-ing a video camera. Thirty seconds. Go!'

Meg looked wonderingly up into Rob's face and found kind eyes, gently teasing. Eyes that were promising her a miracle. . .

This was crazy. This was a man like Meg had never met and she didn't know what on earth he was talking about. Those teasing eyes said quite clearly that he wouldn't tell her. She would just have to trust him.

To trust. . . Meg was quite crazy to trust this man. To go with him, searching for a miracle.

But the gentle eyes were compelling.

And Meg went.

It seemed that the impending miracle was in the stables behind the house.

As Meg reappeared, clad slightly more respectably now with slippers on her feet and a big woollen cardigan over her night attire—all the respectability she could manage in the thirty seconds Rob had demanded—Rob took her hand and led her out of the house without a word.

Meg hesitated as his fingers met hers, but Rob wasn't asking. He was taking.

It was as if Rob was deepening the sense of wonder he'd promised, and his tactics worked. The night was still and warm, the sound of the surf permeated the farmyard and the sky was alight with stars. Rob's dogs met them as they emerged from the house and trotted behind them as protective shadows in the night. Magic. . .

Rob led Meg unresistingly across to the stable door, paused at the entrance to flick on the lamps and then guided her through the numbered stalls.

There were horses at home here—four or five velvety noses pushing enquiringly over the boxes and twitching in recognition as Rob passed with his lady of the night.

His lady of the night. . .

That was how Meg was feeling. Surreal. Floating. As if she'd been lifted and transported to another time entirely.

Another world. . .

In this strange new world there was only the smell of salt air, mingling with the tang of clean straw and the scent of well-groomed horses—and there was only the feel of Rob's hand, guiding her on. She let her hand lie in his with total trust, and a part of her wondered at herself as she did. Crazy sensations. A night out of time. . .

And then Rob pushed open the last box door and held the lantern high, and Meg saw his impending miracle.

There was a mare in the box—a dappled grey mare, no longer young—and she was clearly distressed. She was circling in agitation in the box, and as she circled Meg could see why she was distressed. Her stocky frame was distended with pregnancy—and between the vulval lips was the unmistakable appearance of the shiny white amniotic sac. She was very close to delivery.

'Hey, she's further forward than I thought,' Rob said softly. 'I hadn't expected this so fast. Hey, Mildred. . .'

The old horse looked pleadingly across to him, and Meg could see total trust in the pain-filled eyes. A woman in labour welcoming her obstetrician with relief. . .

Meg didn't move. She could guess how important it must be not to disturb a mare at this stage, so Meg stood uncertainly at the door as Rob moved forward. The dogs also stayed back, well trained and respectful of a lady's right to privacy.

'Meg, can you climb the partition?' Rob asked, still keeping his voice a soft, reassuring murmur as he trod carefully round the hay-strewn stable. There was a bucket of soapy water at one side of the stall. Without waiting for Meg to reply, Rob soaped his arms and turned to examine his patient.

He'd be making sure that the head and front hooves were engaged correctly, Meg thought. Not so different from human patients, only humans didn't have sharp little hooves. . .

'The. . .the partition?' she whispered, trying to figure out just what he was asking.

'That's right.' Rob was intent on his work. As the next contraction eased he swiftly felt the birth canal, and grunted in satisfaction at what his fingers told him.

'Quick, girl,' he ordered Meg. 'I've brought the video camera—it's beside you there. The partition is the only place you'll be able to film from without disturbing Mildred. Climb if you can but, for heaven's sake, don't fall off.'

'I might,' Meg said dubiously, eyeing the wooden barrier with misgiving.

'You'll startle Mildred if you do.' Rob's concern was obviously all for his precious horse. 'Just be careful. Put the camera round your neck as you climb. It's fully automatic. Point it and film until there's nothing left to film.'

Meg looked at the camera. She'd never operated one of these in her life. Then she looked at the partition wall. It was five feet high. It would be no ladylike action to hitch her nightdress above her knees and haul herself up on the partition with a camera dangling round her neck.

But Rob was no longer paying attention. The mare was dropping to the straw, grunting in pain as she rolled from one side to the other, and Rob was kneeling behind her. All his attention was on this birth—and he'd asked Meg to film it.

'So film it,' Meg told herself grimly.

She took a deep breath, slung the camera round her neck, hoisted herself up on a hay bale and then hauled herself higher. Finally she was straddled uncomfortably on the wooden partition, the thin wooden rail providing a most uncomfortable seat. Here she was out of eye contact with the labouring mare but in full view of the birth.

She was also in the view of other horses. On the other side of the rail a small black horse stared up at Meg in amazement. He clattered to the other side of the stall with haste—and stayed there. I'm getting away from the weirdo, his look said, and Meg didn't blame him one bit.

She had work to do. With an apologetic grin at the

startled black horse, she turned her attention back to the labouring mare. Trying not to wobble on her precarious perch, she lifted the camera.

'Film until there's nothing left to film,' Rob had said.

So Meg raised the video camera to her eye and pointed to where Rob's hands were still ensuring that the foal's feet were in position and not catching high and pushing through into the rectum. Somehow she found the red button, and started to film.

She filmed for almost an hour.

For all of that time Rob didn't speak. He stayed crouched behind the mare, making his presence as unobtrusive as possible as the mare successfully delivered her foal into the straw.

Nothing was said to Meg—but she kept filming.

She filmed the tiny nose coming clear, the mare's massive effort as a perfect foal was delivered—to lie in a crumpled heap on the straw—and she filmed as Rob swiftly cleared the airway and gave Meg—or the camera—a triumphant grin as the foal started to breathe on its own.

She filmed as the mare lay still and exhausted on the straw and the newborn foal tried over and over to find its feet. She filmed Rob carefully watching—not interfering but readjusting the straw after every failed attempt to rise so that the foal would always have a soft place to land when its spindly newborn legs folded.

And then Meg filmed the magic moment when the foal struggled gamely once again to its feet—and stayed upright. She filmed it struggling forward, seemingly all head and legs and very little body—but perfectly beautiful, for all its awkwardness.

Meg filmed the mare rising as well, heaving herself upright in her new role as mother. She filmed the old mare nuzzling her fragile newborn foal, pushing it by its still-damp rear quarters so that its tiny muzzle found her swollen teats—and Meg filmed as the foal latched on and drank.

Meg filmed it all, and if at times her eyes were damp behind the camera, well, no one could see. Only Meg knew how much this wondrous, simple picture affected her. She'd seen births before—human births—but there was something about this. . . Something about the tableau of mare and foal—and Rob looking for all the world like he had his miracle.

And finally Rob started clearing up, still moving softly through the stall with careful, measured movements designed not to startle. Then, as Meg released the red button and let the camera finally drop from her face, Rob stepped up on her hay bale, reached high and caught Meg by the waist. He lifted her safely her down, taking his precious camera back into his own care as he did.

'Did you get it all?' he asked softly, and Meg nodded.

'I think so. I certainly hope I did.'

Rob smiled and turned back, watching in satisfaction the mare and foal now peacefully together as one.

And Meg looked wonderingly up at Rob.

This foal was perfect. This birth had been perfect— but it was still an ordinary foaling. Surely, as a country vet, this man must deal often with foalings.

No matter how many human births Meg witnessed it was always a miracle, but there'd been wonder in Rob's voice as he'd led Meg here and wonder as he'd delivered the foal—a wonder that told her this was no ordinary foal.

Rob looked down at Meg, and he saw the question in her eyes even before she asked it.

'This is a very special old horse, Meg,' Rob told her, gesturing to the ageing mare with his face etched with pleasure and satisfaction. 'Mildred belongs to an elderly couple who live just north of here. They think the sun shines out of Mildred, but a couple of months ago Mildred was shot.'

'Shot!' Meg looked up at the mare in horror. 'Who on earth. . .?'

'Spotlighters,' Rob said grimly. He walked slowly forward to run his hand over the mare's flank and Meg saw how the surface was dreadfully scarred. 'We suffer stupid louts from the city who come along the coast, spotlighting, and after a few beers they shoot anything that moves. They shot Mildred late one night and left her lying in the paddock.

'When I was called Mildred was very close to death. I thought. . . Well, given her age, I advised putting her down but her owners, Frank and Ethel Simpson, wouldn't hear of it. The mare was heavy with foal even then. The couple have spent every moment of their time here with her—keeping her on her feet long after I was saying she'd have to be destroyed.

'It's sheer love that's brought Mildred this far, and they'll be so pleased with this outcome.'

There was emotion in Rob's voice as he spoke and once again Meg found herself wondering at Dr Rob Daniels. There was gentleness and caring in this man that she'd never known before.

'It's such a shame they couldn't have been here for the birth themselves,' Meg whispered. She crossed cautiously to fondle behind the foal's damp little ears and silently laughed as the mare nosed her aside to do her own fondling.

'Frank spent a bit too much time here,' Rob told her. 'Both Frank and Ethel are well into their seventies—and Frank's cold turned to pneumonia so he's ended up in the local hospital.' Rob's face clouded. 'I don't think. . . Well, there's a new GP in town who didn't take Frank's illness seriously. Frank's still in hospital, and Ethel won't drive at night so she's missed out on the birth. But. . .'

'But?' Meg looked curiously up at him and Rob smiled.

'But, thanks to you, Dr Preston, we now have it all on film. I hope. I'll check it and, provided you haven't filmed me from my worst angle or photographed the ceiling instead of the horse, I'll take the film into the hospital in the morning.' He put out a hand to draw Meg out of the stable. 'Speaking of which. . .'

'Yes?'

Rob looked doubtfully down at her, his hand still linked in hers. Meg gave her hand a gentle tug away— but the tug was ignored.

'I wondered whether you might like to come with me. To the hospital, I mean.'

'Why would I like to come to the hospital?' Meg's voice was still a whisper. It seemed wrong to speak out loud in this place of peace. Just as it seemed wrong to put too much effort into wrenching her hand away.

There was a long moment of silence and then Rob sighed.

'Because I think I might know who owns your dog.'

More silence.

'You think you might know who owns Spud?' Meg asked at last. Meg did withdraw her hand then and the withdrawal left her feeling oddly alone.

'That's what I said.' Rob ushered Meg out of the stall, closing the door carefully after him. Together they walked back out into the night. 'It's a guess, that's all— but not a crazy guess for all that.'

'Can I ask who it is you think might own him?'

Rob hesitated, walking slowly across the stable yard with his dogs at his heels as he thought out his answer.

'As I said, I'm not sure but. . . Spud's been neutered. His ear's tattooed and the hair round his neck's flattened as if he's worn a collar for most of his life. There's also scar tissue on one of his ears and it looks as if it's been stitched—not all that long ago either. Maybe less than twelve months. I thought I'd read in Sam Fraser's case notes of a dog who fitted that description, and while Mildred was in labour tonight I checked again. Sam Fraser's the vet I replaced six months ago, and his description of the wound and dog fits Spud exactly.'

'I see. . .' Meg looked up at him, vaguely puzzled. 'You only came here six months ago, then?'

'That's right,' Rob told her, and something in his voice prevented further questions. 'Anyway, as I said, I might have found you an owner. Will that solve your problems—or just make more?'

'I'm not sure,' Meg said cautiously. They'd now reached the verandah again. Meg pulled her big jacket about her as if she were cold—but in reality it wasn't coldness which was making her cling to the security of her cardigan. She was overwhelmingly aware of this man's presence beside her.

'I could be wrong,' Rob admitted. 'But, well, Sam had to sew the ear almost completely back after a pit-bull attack and there can't be many wounds like that. The dog in Sam's notes is owned by one Elaine McKechnie— an old lady who lived over the ridge from here. I'd heard she was put in the nursing-home section of the hospital a few months ago.'

'And no one's checked on her dog?' Meg asked incredulously, and Rob shook his head.

'I don't know. I only know of Elaine because one of the farmers mentioned that her farm was empty and dere-lict. I'd assumed her animals had been taken care of long since. Maybe Spud was overlooked.'

'Spud. . .' Meg looked up at him. 'That's his name. You knew. . .'

'As I said, I guessed but I didn't think it'd hurt to suggest Spud as a name before we confirmed it.'

'I see,' Meg said slowly. 'And if Spud's really her dog. . .'

'Then you might still get to keep him.' Both Meg and Rob had stopped beside the verandah steps, as if what they were saying should best be said outside. As it was, Meg thought gratefully. She didn't want Eve to hear this. Even the dogs had gone—back to their kennels, with the excitement of the night deemed over. 'From what I've heard,' Rob continued, 'Mrs McKechnie's a long-term patient. Even if Spud does turn out to be her dog he'll still be in need of a home. So. . . You might still have a problem. Or a dog. Or both.'

'I guess. . .' Meg looked out at the night, her face troubled, and Rob's big hand came down on her shoulder.

'Let's not worry about it tonight, though,' he said gently, and at the gentleness in his voice Meg flushed. The feel of his hand on her shoulder sent strange sensations running right through Meg's body and there was an almost overwhelming compulsion to give in to them. To draw herself closer.

Instead, she pulled herself firmly back, a shiver running though her body as she did.

'You're cold,' Rob said. 'I shouldn't have made you stay out so long.'

'I loved filming the birth,' Meg told him. 'I'm not cold.'

'Nervous, then?'

He saw too much, this vet. This vet with the all-seeing eyes.

'Of. . .of course not,' Meg whispered. 'But. . .I guess I'm tired.'

'And settled enough to sleep now?' Rob asked her gently, and Meg flinched. How on earth was she to answer a question like that?

'I. . .I guess.'

'How long have you been in Australia?' Rob asked,

and Meg relaxed a little. This was easier.

'Six weeks. Eve and I have been travelling round. . .'

'Searching for a miracle cure?'

Meg shrugged. 'Yes,' she admitted. 'I just hoped. . .
Well, what Eve needs is a family. I thought maybe by
the time we went back to England she'd have accepted
me as it.'

'You and Paul. . .'

'Yes. Paul and me.' Meg took a deep breath. 'Look. . .
Dr Daniels. . .'

'Rob.'

'Dr Daniels,' Meg said firmly. 'Thank you. Thank you
for your interest but. . . Well, you've been great but I
have to go to bed.'

'So you do,' Rob said gently and, before Meg could
ward him off, he lifted a hand and ran a strong, firm
finger down the smoothness of her cheek. 'And I know.
It's none of my business. It's just I see so many shadows
hanging over you. . . Too many for one slip of a girl
to cope with on her own and I'd like the opportunity
to help.'

'You can't see that,' Meg whispered. 'You. . .I mean,
you've only known me for a few hours.'

'Have I?' Rob asked in a strange voice. 'Have I? You
know, Meg, it feels much longer. It feels as if I've known
you for a long, long time. Somehow. . . But. . .' He drew
his hand away and took a step back. 'Maybe you're right,
Dr Preston. Maybe you should go to bed right now—
before I'm tempted to know you even better.'

Meg gasped.

She took a step back as well, and stood staring up at
him in the moonlight. Their eyes locked.

And it was just as Rob had said. It was as. . .as if there
was something between them that had always been there,
and always would.

And it scared Meg to death.

She lifted her hand to her face where Rob had touched her and opened her lips as if to speak—but no sound came.

'Go to bed, Meg,' Rob said gently. 'Go to bed and sleep. Face whatever has to be faced in the morning, but not before. All you have to do tonight is sleep.'

All. . .

All Meg had to do was turn and walk away from this man, who was looking down into her face with such tenderness and wonder that Meg wanted to weep.

And turning and walking away was the hardest thing Meg had ever done in her life.

CHAPTER FIVE

DESPITE her confusion, Meg slept, and if dreams of injured dogs and troubled cousins were somehow interspersed with the image of one enigmatic veterinary surgeon it wasn't to be wondered at. The sun was well up when she finally woke.

Rob Daniels was already at work. Meg lay in bed and listened to the sound of his early morning household. There was the sound of a kettle whistling in the kitchen, footsteps along the passage and back again—a barking from outside, mingling with bird calls of kookaburra and magpie, and then the sound of an older female voice from the direction of the kitchen. The woman's voice was rich with laughter as it mingled with Rob's deeper tones.

She couldn't stay in bed any longer. Meg checked on a still-sleeping Eve, showered, donned shorts and blouse and took herself to the kitchen.

The kitchen had been taken over. A middle-aged lady of vast proportions, robed in an amazing flowered caftan, was presiding over the stove, and wonderful smells were everywhere.

'You must be the new doctor,' the lady beamed as Meg appeared at the door. 'Well, you don't look much like a doctor, that's for sure, but Dr Daniels says you're just that so I'll take his word for it. Sit yourself down and get some scrambled eggs inside you.'

This wasn't a lady to be argued with. Meg sat down gingerly, a large plate was placed before her and the lady started preparing another.

'I was about to bring this to you in bed,' the lady told her. 'Now you're up you can have breakfast here, but

I'll take this in to your little cousin. Dr Daniels told me all about her and I can't wait to try my hand at feeding her up. If this doesn't do the job. . .'

'Eve doesn't eat much. . .' Meg started and then paused. The plate of scrambled eggs in front of Meg was generous in the extreme, but the plate the woman was preparing for Eve was different.

It held golden buttered toast triangles with the crusts removed, a small mound of creamy scrambled eggs lying enticingly within the triangles and slivers of tomato to the side. The plate was garnished with tiny crisp leaves of fragrant basil, and its elegant presentation was enough to tempt the most fussy of eaters. Maybe Eve would. . .

'You don't need to worry,' the lady beamed. 'I've done my fill of invalid cooking and I know there's nought worse than having a great plateful when you're not sure whether you want to eat at all. A little often, I always say, when you're feeling poorly, and if the mite needs feeding—like Doc Daniels says—then I'm just your lady. Now you wrap yourself round your own breakfast while I take this in.'

And she was gone, with Meg staring almost open-mouthed after her. She made to rise and then sat helplessly down again. Maybe this vast whirlwind could win where Meg was so miserably failing.

She could.

The woman was gone for fifteen minutes and when she returned it was with an empty plate and a beam almost as wide as her face.

'Now, what did I say? She's eaten every scrap, and I doubt she even noticed she was eating. I chatted to her the whole time and I'm sure she was too intent on my caftan to think about food. She's showering now because Doc Daniels wants her to look after the little dog while he takes you into the hospital.'

Meg took a deep breath and laid down her knife and

fork. Like Eve, she had polished off a good breakfast but there were questions which needed to be answered.

'You seem to know all about us,' she started cautiously. 'But. . . Well, may I ask who you are?'

If it was possible for the beam to widen, it widened then.

'Didn't I tell you? I'm sorry, lass. I'm Maggie Mewett, Doc Daniels's housekeeper, answering service and animal minder. I'm here most weekdays. Doc Daniels has a vet nurse who's here for surgery but I do everything else.' Maggie poured Meg a mug of coffee, poured one for herself and lowered herself with caution onto a kitchen chair. The chair almost audibly groaned.

'And where's Dr Daniels?' Meg managed, and her question was answered from the door.

'At your service.'

Rob.

Meg turned to face Rob Daniels, and for the life of her she couldn't help the tinge of crimson rising swiftly over her face. Maggie's sharp eyes flew from Meg to Rob with avid interest and Meg's colour only increased.

Rob had obviously been working. He wore a white clinical coat over his jeans, and if it wasn't for the heavy leather work boots on his feet he could almost be taken for a doctor in a hospital. Apart, that is, from the three dogs at his heels, bounding in to welcome Maggie with the enthusiasm of all dogs for a really excellent cook.

'Has Maggie been looking after you?' Rob asked. He smiled, pouring himself a coffee and pulling up a chair. The sun streaming through the window glinted on his red-brown hair and reflected in the smile he was directing straight at Meg.

'A-absolutely.' Meg fought her colour down, retreating into the safety of her coffee-mug. When she finally emerged Rob's eyes were still smiling, and the colour started rising all over again.

'You look better for your sleep,' he told her approvingly, his eyes resting on her flushed face and her mass of tumbled curls. Meg had brushed them but had left them hanging free round her shoulders in her haste to reach the kitchen. Now she felt an overwhelming urge to tie them back in a knot—a very severe knot.

She moved uncomfortably on the chair—and the hawk-eyed Rob noted the movement.

'Problem?' His eyes creased downward.

'No.'

'You're a liar, Meg Preston,' he said easily. 'You forget I'm accustomed to diagnosing patients who can't tell me what's wrong. Why are you acting as if my kitchen chair is too hard?'

'Because it is,' Meg said with asperity. 'If you push me to climb thin wooden walls and sit on a ledge less than half an inch wide. . .'

'Oh-ho. . .' Rob's smile broadened again. 'A diagnosis of painful posterior, is it? I'm sorry, Meg.'

'There's no need,' Meg admitted. 'I enjoyed it so much I hardly noticed the discomfort. But I do have a splinter or two for my pains.'

'Now you can't leave them there. Would you like me to help remove them?' Rob asked innocently, and Meg flushed all over again.

'I would not,' she managed. She cast an appealing glance at Maggie. 'But maybe after breakfast if Maggie could. . .'

'There's nothing I'm better at than wielding tweezers and iodine,' Maggie beamed and she looked severely at Rob. 'Don't you get any funny ideas about helping, Dr Daniels, my lad. There are some places where vets just aren't wanted.'

Rob's bit his lips together, suppressing laughter, and turned his attention to his coffee.

'If you don't want me then I'll retire to a corner and

sulk,' he said sadly. 'My professional pride is wounded to the core. However. . . If this operation can be performed quickly—I'm driving into town in half an hour.' The smile returned. 'If you can still sit down will you come into the hospital with me then?'

Meg glanced at her watch. Nine o'clock! Somehow, despite her tension, she'd still managed to sleep late.

'Don't you have surgery?' she asked.

'I've had surgery,' he smiled. 'All done. Nice and quiet for a Sunday morning. I discovered early that by running surgery early on Sunday morning I only get major problems. Minor problems wait until weekdays. However. . . I've stitched the leg of one idiotic Dalmatian who tried to climb a barbed wire fence when the gate was open six feet away, and I've treated the infected eye of an elderly Persian cat. Hardly stirring stuff. I wouldn't mind adding splinter removal to my list.'

'I. . .I imagined your practice would be more rural,' Meg queried, still blushing. 'You're so far from town.'

'Only four miles and Gundowring doesn't have anyone else. During the week I run a clinic in town for everyone who can't drive out here but I prefer to work from home—especially at the weekend.'

'I don't blame you,' Meg smiled. 'I'm amazed you could ever have borne to leave this place while you did your training.' Then she hesitated as Rob's smile slipped.

'As you say,' he said shortly, and rose to pour himself another coffee.

Meg frowned. For all this man seemed so transparent—so open and friendly—there were shadows round him that she couldn't see a cause for.

'Will you come into the hospital?' Rob asked again curtly, and Meg rose too.

'Yes. If. . .if Maggie could help me now I'll put a dress on after splinter removal. If I'm about to approach an old lady to ask for her dog. . .'

'It'd be good if you looked a bit older than twelve,' Rob agreed, his eyes raking Meg's slim figure with obvious appreciation. The humour crept back behind his eyes.

'I. . .I'll tell Eve where I'm going,' Meg managed, trying desperately to ignore the blatant admiration in Rob's look. 'Eve can come with us.'

'Eve's staying here,' Rob said firmly. 'I've just visited the young lady while she was engaged in breakfast and we've agreed she's in charge of Spud while we're away. Maggie will take care of Eve.'

'I don't. . .' Meg looked doubtfully across at Maggie. 'I don't think. . .'

'You don't think she'll be safe with me?' The housekeeper shook her head. 'You're out there, lass.' The woman's face softened and she cast a doubtful look at Rob. 'A. . .a friend of mine had a daughter with this anorexia business and I've been through it before. You're afraid Eve'll make herself sick while she's with me— get rid of her breakfast. Well, maybe she's doing that now but I doubt it. She's been given a job to do and I'll keep on giving her jobs so she's so busy she won't even think about her stomach. Trust me, dear. I can keep as close an eye on her as you.'

Meg bit her lip. She looked from Maggie to Rob and back again. These two were lifting her burden and she could only be grateful.

'I'll be quick,' she told them, and made her escape before either could see the tears pricking out from behind her lashes.

'I'll find some tweezers and be with you in a tick,' Maggie called after her. 'And save your tears for after splinter removal—not before.'

Her escape had not been fast enough. It seemed that Meg was incapable of hiding anything from these two.

*   *   *

'I'll find a hotel while we're in town,' Meg told Rob on their ride into town. 'We can't stay with you for another night.'

'Why on earth not?'

Rob drove well, his hands light on the wheel of his Land Rover and his eyes on the road ahead, but he still watched the girl at his side.

For all her misgivings, Meg was enjoying the ride. The Land Rover's hood was down; the warm sea air was making her shoulder-length curls fly out behind her. Her light sun-dress was a soft, gay print. She felt pretty and warm and blessedly free from tension. On holiday. . .

Indeed she was. She was on holiday from responsibility.

It would be easy to let this continue, she thought fleetingly. It would be so easy to let Rob keep lifting her burden.

Easy, but dangerous. . .

'We need to be on our own,' Meg managed firmly. 'Eve and I.'

'Being on your own hasn't worked so far,' Rob told her. 'Why not let Maggie and me lend a hand?'

'Because we must learn to be on our own.' Meg's voice was flat and definite. There was no long-term answer for Eve in staying with Rob and Maggie. Surely Rob could see that?

It seemed he couldn't.

He looked across at Meg thoughtfully, raised his eyebrows in a mock query—and then concentrated on the road. Meg was left to make of his thoughts as she would.

Gundowring Hospital was the most beautiful little hospital Meg had ever seen.

Like Rob's home, the hospital was built out on a headland just through the town. Built of whitewashed stone, with wide verandahs running full length around it and

gardens running down to the sea, it was the sort of building that made you feel better just to look at it. If this
was where the afflicted of Gundowring came to be healed
Meg couldn't imagine a place more suited for healing.

'How many beds does the hospital have?' Meg asked
as they pulled into the car park.

'Thirty.'

Meg's eyes widened. Surely Gundowring wasn't a big
enough town to support such a hospital.

'There are twenty nursing-home beds as well,' Rob
assured her. 'The nearest major hospital from here is five
hours' drive, so we service a fair district. We have a
good band of specialists. The local joke is that any time
we need another medical speciality we just get one of
the locals to propose marriage. Works a treat.'

Meg flashed Rob a suspicious look—but Rob met her
look blandly.

'You don't need to worry, Dr Preston,' he said mildly.
'We don't have a vacancy for a general practitioner. At
least—I don't think we have.'

'How. . .how very fortunate,' Meg managed, and
swung herself out of the car with her colour rising.

Rob led her though the hospital grounds as if he knew
them well.

'It's just on ten,' he explained. 'If we're lucky we
might catch most of the medical staff at morning tea. On
Sunday morning they have an informal practice meeting
after ward rounds and I'd like to introduce you. The GP
treating Elaine McKechnie may well be there.'

'You know the doctors?' Meg asked curiously as they
walked side by side, and Rob nodded.

'I call on them for help,' he explained. 'Often. Being
a solo vet has its drawbacks and if I'm doing an extensive
or tricky operation the surgeon or anaesthetist will often
lend a hand.'

'But. . . If Gundowring's big enough to support a large

hospital why isn't it large enough to support two vets?'

'It's certainly large enough,' Rob smiled as they walked. 'But, with so many mountains between here and a major city, it's almost impossible to attract professionals. As I said, the major inducement seems to be marriage. What a shame you're a human doctor.'

Rob hesitated and a look came into his eyes which Meg couldn't understand. He closed his eyes for a fleeting moment, as though fighting some inner conflict. 'A real shame,' he repeated finally. 'But enough of that.' Before she could realise what he intended, Rob took her hand as they reached a door at the end of the nearest building. 'Let's get you introduced and find you a dog owner, Dr Preston,' he told her gently. 'We'll worry about finding me another vet later.'

Meg stared down at their linked hands.

She gave her hand a futile tug as he led her on, but that was all it was—futile. Finally she gave up on the attempt. Meg Preston was starting to realise that where Rob Daniels led he expected her to follow.

The meeting of Gundowring's doctors was, it seemed, taking place in the hospital kitchen.

The kitchen was crowded—filled with white coats and laughter and the smell of fresh brewed coffee. Meg's arrival was met with undisguised curiosity and a very definite welcome as she was introduced to the town's medical contingent.

'Welcome to Gundowring, Dr Preston. Hey, Rob. . .' The hospital director, Struan Maitland, was bouncing an energetic toddler on his knee as he greeted his friend and Meg. 'You're just the man we need. A babysitter to take away our encumbrances while we talk business.'

'If you and Gina keep producing encumbrances, then you and Gina get to look after them,' Rob grinned, his eyes taking in the tribe of little ones cruising round under the table while their parents tried to talk medicine. 'This looks like a play group rather than a hospital meeting. I should have brought a pup or two instead of Meg.'

'We're glad you brought Meg instead.' Struan's wife, Gina, an attractive young woman with stethoscope dangling from her breast pocket and a teddy bear under her arm, rose and took Meg's hand in a friendly grip. 'These don't all belong to Struan and me, Meg, despite Rob's comments about our fecundity.

'The twins belong to Lloyd and Sally—Lloyd's our anaesthetist and Sally here is our general surgeon—and the little girl with Vegemite on her face belongs to Martin. Martin's our orthopaedic surgeon and his wife just happens to be our hospital matron. Welcome to Gundowring, Dr Preston.'

As she spoke Gina's friendly eyes went from Rob to Meg, asking all sorts of unvoiced questions. Despite the questioning eyes, there was no mistaking the pleasure all the doctors here felt in seeing Rob Daniels with an attractive woman by his side. Meg could feel her colour rising at their obvious interest.

'There's a reason I brought Meg,' Rob explained, ignoring the unasked questions in Gina's eyes. He poured coffee and ushered Meg into a chair at the end of the table. 'We're wondering who's looking after Elaine McKechnie.'

'Elaine McKechnie. . .' Gina turned to her husband. 'Isn't Elaine one of Geoff's nursing-home patients?'

'Yes.' Struan placed his coffee-cup back down on the table with a definite clunk, and for the first time a hint of unease spread over the room. 'What's the problem?'

'Meg's found Elaine's dog.' Rob swiftly outlined Spud's story and the faces round the table tightened.

'Geoff knew Elaine had animals there,' Gina whispered. 'He said things were under control. I asked him if he needed a social worker and he said she didn't need one. He said she had her affairs in order.'

'Geoff wouldn't have brought in a social worker if he could help it.' Sally, the surgeon at the far end of the table, was staring down at the table in disgust. Even though the young surgeon was staring at scrubbed wood, Meg could tell that in her mind's eye she was seeing something—or someone—she disliked intensely. 'He'd have had to contact Melbourne and write a referral.'

'Sally. . .' Struan's voice was gently reproving but the young woman wasn't so easily silenced. Struan turned to Meg. 'Geoff's a GP with some geriatric training. He's in charge of nursing-home patients.'

'In charge. . . Struan, we all know the man's nothing but a lazy oaf,' the young surgeon retorted, supremely unabashed by the medical director's reproof. 'Geoff was brought here on six months' approval to act as part-time nursing home medico and part-time GP and as far as we can see he's acted like a part-time doctor in total.

'He's been here five months, and he's been here for five months too long, in my opinion. He's been a disaster while you've been away. Heaven knows the damage he's done because the rest of us have been too busy to keep tabs on him. I vote we pay him off and get rid of him.'

'And replace him with whom?' Struan said heavily. 'Doctors here are hardly thick on the ground.'

'Well, we have one looking at us,' Sally smiled, her anger fading as she looked back to Meg. 'Rob did say you were a doctor, didn't he, Meg? I suppose there's no way. . .?'

'No way!' Meg pushed herself to her feet, suddenly seeing chasms yawning in front of her—black and bottomless. 'I'm here on holiday. In a day or two I'll be leaving. . .'

The surgeon's eyes swung to Rob, brightly questioning, and—like Meg—Rob also rose to his feet.

'No, you don't, Dr Atchinson,' he grinned. 'Any matchmaking to be done will be done by me and only me. Besides, I need another vet.' He hesitated, and was it Meg's imagination or did the smile slip a little? 'And there'll be no matchmaking until I find someone who likes treating Shetland ponies.'

There was a shout of general laughter, in which Meg joined a little self-consciously. She'd reacted stupidly to what was no more than teasing.

'Are you sure that's not just an excuse, though, Rob?' Sally asked as the laughter died, and suddenly the room was tense.

'Sally!' Gina spoke sharply and Sally flushed.

'I'm sorry, Rob,' she said contritely. She smiled beseechingly at the vet. 'It's just I think Meg's smashing and we need another doctor. . .'

The laughter and talk started again but the tension stayed, for all the good-humoured banter.

There was something behind Rob Daniels beside laughter and kindness, Meg decided, casting him an uneasy sideways glance. What? A tragedy? Shadows. . . They were subtle but they were definitely there, for all that.

'Can I visit Mrs McKechnie?' she asked, cutting across the raillery, and the medical director's smile faded with the laughter round the table.

'Sure, Meg,' Struan told her. 'She's in the nursing home part of the hospital. Would you like me to take you to her?'

'I'll take her,' Rob said shortly, and by his tone Meg realised that for him as well the raillery was becoming a strain. He laughed at himself, did Rob, but the shadows lay deep just the same.

'OK, Rob. If you find Geoff Cooper send him over with a flea in his ear, will you?' Struan asked. 'He should be here.' He turned back to the notes on the table and nodded his farewell.

*   *   *

The nursing home was a separate wing, surrounded by gardens. Meg and Rob walked through rows of neatly tended vegetables as the air of constraint between them deepened.

'I'm sorry about that crew,' Rob said at last. 'It's a bit much to hit you with job offers the moment you arrive.'

'It's a compliment, I guess,' Meg managed lightly. 'They mustn't be all that fond of this Geoff.'

'Geoff Cooper's a lazy slob,' Rob told her. 'But, as they said, it's hard to find doctors prepared to move this far from the city. We take what we can find.'

They didn't speak to each other again until they found Elaine McKechnie.

Elaine was easy to find.

'She's still in bed,' the nurse in charge told them. She flashed Rob a worried glance. 'Dr Daniels. . .I didn't know you knew Mrs McKechnie.'

'I don't,' Rob told her shortly. 'Dr Preston here wants to see her on personal business.'

'Oh.' The nurse cast Meg a glance which was distinctly nervous. 'Are you a doctor?'

'She's a real one,' Rob smiled. 'A people one, not like me. Can we see her?'

'Well, yes,' the nurse said dubiously. 'But I don't know how much sense you'll get from her. She was too ill to dress this morning. I've asked Dr Cooper to come and see her but he hasn't done his rounds yet.'

'What's wrong with her?' Meg asked.

The nurse simply shrugged. She looked at them both again, her face clouding in doubt, and then finally, silently, led them down the corridor and opened a bedroom door.

'I'm not sure what's wrong,' she answered at last. 'Mrs McKecknie, you have visitors. Are you well enough to see them?'

The mound under the bedclothes hardly responded. The nurse walked forward and pulled back the sheet, revealing a tiny crinkled face on the white pillows. The woman was in real trouble, Meg thought. There were beads of sweat on her face, but her lips and mouth looked parchment-dry. The old woman raised a hand in a feeble response to the nurse but it trembled so much that she laid it down again.

There was a chart on the end of the bed. Meg couldn't help herself. Professional curiosity couldn't be contained. She walked over and lifted the chart—and frowned. The chart read like the chart of someone in Intensive Care.

'Mrs McKechnie's temperature's been up for forty-eight hours,' she said slowly. 'And her blood pressure is all over the place.'

'Maybe her temp's been up for longer,' the nurse told her. 'We don't keep charts unless there's a reason. On Friday morning she couldn't eat breakfast and had a fall on the way back to her bedroom. The nurse on duty started the chart then.'

'And what does Dr Cooper say?'

'Nothing,' the nurse said stiffly. 'He hasn't seen her.'

'He hasn't. . .' Meg hung the chart gently back on the bed-end and stared at the nurse in stupefaction. 'What do you mean? He hasn't seen her since Friday?'

'I. . . Well, we contacted him on Friday of course,' the nurse managed. 'He said he'd come when he had time. We rang him again last night—see, we noted it on the chart—but he wasn't answering his pager. So we thought we'd just better keep on with the chart.'

'To cover yourself,' Meg said grimly. The nurse here had done exactly what she was supposed to do and no more. 'If Dr Cooper hasn't had time to visit surely you could have contacted someone else?' Meg's voice was grim to the point of anger. She bit her lip. 'There are six other doctors drinking coffee not two hundred yards away from here right now.'

'The nursing-home patients are Dr Cooper's responsibility,' the nurse said unhappily. 'He gets furious if we contact any of the other doctors.' She cast an uncertain glance at the old lady, huddled in the bed. 'He always comes in on Monday morning.'

'You don't have until Monday morning.'

Meg's meaning was absolutely clear both to the nurse and to Rob, still standing beside her. Meg placed her hand on the old lady's wrist and winced. The pulse was faint and fast. The skin was so dry to touch that it seemed almost flaky. The old lady looked up to Meg and opened her lips to speak, but no sound came out.

Meg hesitated for all of two seconds. It wasn't her place to interfere—but what was happening here was nothing short of criminal.

'When did she last drink?' she snapped.

'I don't know.' The nurse was frightened now, fearing blame. 'The kitchen staff brought her meals but I don't know if she ate them.'

'No, I don't suppose you do,' Meg muttered. She stooped so that her eyes were now on a level with the old lady's frightened ones. 'Mrs McKechnie, I'm a doctor and, if you agree, I'd like to make you more comfortable. Is that OK with you?' Then, at the look of relief flashing into the tired old eyes, Meg rose again. 'I want a saline drip set up and I want it now.'

'I can't put up a drip without Dr Cooper's say-so,' the girl muttered.

'Dr Preston can, though,' Rob retorted. His eyes were resting on Elaine McKechnie's frail form, and Meg's anger was reflected in his face. 'She's a Pom, for heaven's sake, and isn't answerable to any of us colonials.'

'Rob. . .'

'Meg.' Rob's hand came down on Meg's shoulder in a gesture of absolute support. 'What do you want me to do?'

'I want you to fetch one of your coffee-drinking friends from their meeting,' Meg said grimly. 'Drag them here by force, if necessary. You know I'm not registered to practise here. I shouldn't be doing anything but I'm damned if I'll stand aside and let this negligence continue. And if this precious Dr Cooper's available you have my permission to haul him in by the hair. But fast, Rob.'

'I'm on my way, Dr Preston.' Rob's eyes were alight with admiration. 'I'll bring Struan.'

'But. . .' The nurse took Rob's arm and gripped it. 'Please. . . If you have to get someone. . . Dr Cooper's in his flat just down from the hospital. I saw his car there this morning on my way to work. It's just. . .he doesn't like getting up early. You could ring and tell him. . .tell him to come.'

'Like you should have,' Rob retorted.

'He wouldn't have come if I'd called,' the nurse said miserably. 'But he will if you do, and if he comes later and thinks I've called someone else. . .'

'You'll cop it.' Rob's face softened. It seemed that this girl was caught between a rock and a hard place, and Rob Daniels wasn't a judgemental man. 'OK, Sister. I'll try and find Cooper first. It's over to you here, though, Meg. Let's see who works fastest, you or me.'

'I'll have a drip set up by the time you're back,' Meg promised. Then she looked down at Mrs McKechnie's dulling eyes and her heart sank within her. If it wasn't too late already.

CHAPTER SIX

By THE time Rob located Geoff Cooper and propelled him to the hospital Meg had intravenous fluids already running at maximum rate into Elaine McKechnie's dehydrated body.

Meg ordered the nurse to prepare an antibiotic, but Meg left its administration to Cooper. She was unregistered to work in Australia. If she was forced to administer the antibiotic she would, but a few more minutes wouldn't make a difference. Much more time, though, without fluid. . .

She glanced round as the two men came into the room—Rob and a man beside him, who was presumably Cooper. Slowly she turned. Rob's curt introduction was brushed aside as pure irrelevance.

Meg's anger had been building as she worked. She shouldn't be doing this. She hadn't the right to treat other doctors' patients, and it was untenable that Cooper's neglect had forced her into this position. He'd better have a darned good reason.

As soon as Cooper walked in the door, though, Meg knew that she wouldn't get a reason. The man Rob brought back wasn't in the least apologetic or concerned. Geoff Cooper burst into the room in a bluster of rage.

And something else too. The man smelled strongly of alcohol—so strongly that the smell hit Meg almost before he opened his mouth.

'What the hell do you think you're doing?' Cooper demanded of Meg from the doorway—even before Rob had completed his introduction. 'I'll thank you to leave my patients alone.'

'Dr Preston is only assisting where you wouldn't. . .' Rob began, but Meg silenced Rob with her eyes. Rob met Meg's look, held her eyes for a fraction of a moment while he read their silent message and then gave an imperceptible nod. Over to you, his look said.

'This patient needs intravenous antibiotic, Doctor,' Meg said carefully. 'Mrs McKechnie is badly dehydrated and she obviously has some infection. I've set up an emergency IV line to rehydrate. Now, will you administer antibiotic—or will I?'

'What the hell. . .?' The doctor, middle-aged, flabby and unkempt—as if he'd slept in yesterday's clothes or maybe the day before's—walked over to the bed and stared down at Elaine McKechnie. 'Who says she needs antibiotic?' he demanded.

'According to her chart, she's been running a temperature since Friday,' Meg told him, keeping her temper in check with an effort. 'As you'd have known if you'd checked.'

'Oh, for God's sake. . .' The doctor lifted the chart, stared at it and then flung it down onto the bed-cover. The clipboard must have hit the old lady's legs, but Elaine McKechnie was beyond reacting. 'So what if she's running a temperature?' Cooper growled. 'If I came running every time one of these old ducks complained of a fever. . .'

'But she's very ill,' Meg managed, trying desperately to keep her calm. 'She's dreadfully dehydrated. If you're. . .if we're not careful her heart will start to show the strain.'

It already is, Meg thought grimly, though she wouldn't say so while within earshot of the patient. She'd borrowed a stethoscope while Rob was away finding Cooper, and she'd listened. The fluttering, erratic heartbeats told their own story.

'Well, so what?' The doctor folded his arms and stared

at Meg belligerently. 'We're not in a high-tech resuscitation unit here, lady.'

'And what do you mean by that?' Meg's voice was calm all by itself now. Dangerously calm.

'Meaning this woman is over eighty, for heaven's sake,' Cooper snapped. 'If you think I'm racing in to give intravenous antibiotics to every doddery old. . .'

'Sister, is Mrs McKechnie suffering from Alzheimer's disease?' Meg demanded suddenly. 'Is she mentally confused—or does she have some deep-seated, life-threatening and untreatable illness?'

Meg was feeling cold through and through now. Maybe this conversation should be held out of Elaine's hearing but, having gone this far, the woman deserved to know what was happening to her. Dear heaven, if Mrs McKechnie was aware of what Dr Cooper was suggesting. . .

Meg's hand dropped down to take Elaine McKechnie's hand in hers. To her surprise she felt the old fingers respond—curl around her own and grip.

'She's not. . .' The nurse was almost incoherent with fright. She cast an uncertain glance from Geoff Cooper to Meg—and then she looked back to Cooper. Rob's solid presence was right beside the nurse and it seemed to give the girl courage. She took a deep breath—and threw in her lot solidly behind Meg.

'Mrs McKechnie's frail but mentally she's fine,' the nurse managed. 'Until now there's been nothing wrong with her, except for general frailty. She. . .she plays chess with Mr Barret and she nearly always beats him; she gets books from our mobile library twice a week—and she plays the piano for all of us. . .' The nurse's voice trailed off, her defiance fading.

Cooper's breath hissed in with fury and he glared straight at the nurse. If looks could have killed the nurse would be dead on the spot.

No wonder this nurse hadn't wanted to call Cooper, Meg thought. He had the girl terrified. Rob's solid bulk was still beside the nurse, and the girl took a hasty step backward—as if Rob could somehow deflect the fury.

'So. . .so you've decided this woman doesn't warrant treatment,' Meg said slowly, watching Cooper's face turn various shades of puce. 'You've decided it's her time to die. Regardless of the fact that she's still enjoying life. Regardless of the fact that she's your patient and her trust has to be in you.'

Elaine's hand in hers gave Meg the courage to continue. It was a gesture of faith from someone who seemed unutterably alone. Someone who desperately needed a champion to fight her most important battle.

'Look, we don't have the resources. . .'

'You're talking criminal bullshit!' Meg snarled, and flinched inside at her use of the word. She'd never said such a thing in her life—and to say it in front of all these people. . . It didn't matter, though. She was past caring what they thought of her. What Cooper was saying— what this man was doing—demanded expletives of a worse kind than Meg even knew.

'It's criminal,' she said again, grinding her teeth on the word. 'And well you know it, Dr Cooper. What cost is a bag of saline and some antibiotic? What cost? Are you telling me that all these doctors in this hospital feel like you, and you can't afford treatment?

'Are you telling me that you have government approval for euthanasia—because that's what this is, Dr Cooper, only I don't even think this amounts even to mercy killing. I think it amounts to nothing short of murder—to fail to treat an otherwise healthy woman suffering an infection. Now, are you going to administer antibiotics this minute, or will I? You choose—but if you don't treat Mrs McKechnie and treat her now, Dr Cooper, I'll be reporting you to every medical board and government authority I can find in this country. So choose, Dr Cooper. . .'

'I. . .I won't. . . It's none of your damned business.'

The nursing sister had hopefully lifted the tray with what was needed to put the antibiotic into the drip. She stood, waiting, as Cooper glared around the room.

Heaven knew what Dr Cooper intended—Meg certainly didn't—but Cooper's hand came out to take the tray from the nurse. His hand never reached its target. The hand shook with alcoholic weakness, and before the doctor could grip the aluminium surface Rob's hand flew out and knocked his hand aside.

'You're still drunk,' Rob said in disgust. 'Meg, do what you have to do. You must see that Cooper can't treat anyone, no matter what you threaten him with. I never should have brought him near you. I'm sorry, Meg. I didn't realise he was so far gone.'

'How dare you. . .? I am not. . .'

It was Cooper's last bluster. Rob took the back of Cooper's collar in one hand and the seat of his pants in the other—and forcibly ejected the man from the room. Then Rob paused, before following the blustering Cooper. 'Get the antibiotic going, Meg,' he said briefly with a firm, reassuring nod. 'I'll fetch Struan and see this creep doesn't come near you again. Ever!'

And he closed the door behind them.

Meg and the nurse were left staring at each other.

Meg's hand was still in Elaine's. Slowly she turned to look down at the bed.

And there was the faintest trace of a twinkling smile in the tired, weak old eyes. A smile, after all that. . . There must be some strength left in her to enjoy what Rob had done.

'I'm so sorry,' Meg managed, gripping the frail old hand tighter. 'I wouldn't have had this happen for the world. But if it's OK, Mrs McKechnie. . . If you don't mind, I think I might take over for a little.'

The smile deepened. The grip on Meg's hand became a tug, pulling her down against old lips so that Meg could hear the threadlike whisper.

'Please,' whispered Elaine McKechnie, 'please. . . I'd like you for my doctor.'

It took fifteen minutes to do what she could for the old lady—fifteen minutes until Meg was content that there was nothing else she could do to give Elaine McKechnie every chance of recovering. Finally she left Elaine to the ministrations of a suddenly very conscientious nurse, and emerged to find Rob coming in the main entrance doors with Struan Maitland, the medical director, by his side.

'How is she?' Rob asked and Meg shook her head, refusing to meet either Rob's or the medical director's eyes. She walked down the corridor to the nurses' station before she spoke again. What she intended to say she didn't want Mrs McKechnie hearing.

Her temper didn't cool with the waiting, however, and when Meg finally spoke she let go with both barrels.

'Mrs McKechnie's desperately ill,' she told them, finally turning to face both men. Especially the medical director. Her anger was almost palpable, and it was directed straight at Struan Maitland. 'What sort of hospital are you running here, Dr Maitland?' she demanded. 'What this man—your Dr Cooper—has been doing amounts to criminal negligence. The medical ethics doesn't differ so much between our countries that I can't tell gross misconduct when I see it. If you're in charge here then you have quite a case to answer.'

'Meg. . .' Rob's voice cut placatingly across Meg's tirade but Meg was too angry to notice.

'Mrs McKechnie's been running a temp of over thirty-nine since Friday at least,' she told them both. 'There's been no check at all of fluid intake—in fact, I'd say she's had no fluid intake since then. The nurse you have in charge is incompetent and the doctor is worse.

'If you can't run this place better then you should close it down because you're doing no one any favours by leaving it open. Mrs McKechnie would almost be better off out on the street. At least someone then might be concerned enough to give her a glass of water and help her drink it.'

'Meg, it's not Struan's fault. . .' Rob started but Meg flashed straight back over him.

'Oh, yes, it is. If Dr Maitland is the medical director then the behaviour of his staff is directly at his door. If Mrs McKecknie dies then you're liable, Dr Maitland. I'm telling you that now, and I'm also saying that if Elaine has friends able to take her case to court I'll back them every inch of the way. With bells on!'

Meg paused, her anger dissipating in a rush that now left her feeling empty and sick. Poor old woman. . .

And both men were looking at Meg as if they couldn't believe their eyes.

'Meg. . .'

'Dr Preston. . .'

They spoke in unison but it was Rob who stepped forward and placed his arm round Meg's suddenly shaking shoulders. He'd seen almost before Meg realised it herself that her tirade had left her limp at the knees. Meg was no virago. To be so angry was totally out of character—but, then, seldom had she ever had grounds for such anger.

'It's OK, sweetheart,' Rob said gently. He was handling her as if she were Dresden china—a rare and wondrous creature he'd only just learned the value of.

'I'm not. . .' It was suddenly all Meg could do to get her voice to work. 'I'm not your sweetheart.'

'I wish you were attached to Rob.' It was Struan Maitland talking now, his brow black and thunderous.

He motioned Rob to an easy chair in the corner of the sisters' station and Rob gently propelled Meg there. Then, at Rob's look of surprise, he explained his statement. 'I wish you were willing to stay here permanently, Dr Preston. To have someone overseeing these patients who cares as much as you. . . Dr Preston, I can only apologise. . .'

'It needs only that,' Meg whispered bleakly. 'It's not me you should be apologising to. It's Elaine McKechnie.'

'Meg, hear him out.' Rob took Meg's hands and gripped them, stooping so that his eyes were on a level with hers. 'There are things going on you should know before you judge Struan.'

'Like what?' Meg said wearily. 'An epidemic of old people? Too many people for beds, Dr Maitland, so you thought you'd get rid of some? Turn a blind eye to active euthanasia to empty a few beds?'

'That's hardly fair,' Struan Maitland told her, his face still grim. 'But. . .' He hesitated. 'I agree. I take responsibility for what's going on here, though, as Rob says, it's been somewhat out of my control. I've been away. Our second child, Sarah—or Pumpkin as she's more commonly known—is four years old and has had medical problems since birth. She needed a major operation in a specialist children's hospital, so Gina and I have been in Melbourne for six weeks.

'Pumpkin's made a complete recovery, thank God, but this is our first weekend back and I'm just picking up the reins. And everywhere I go I'm starting to be told how bad Cooper is.'

'You employed him in the first place.'

'I did,' Struan said heavily. 'I didn't like the man but his references were impeccable. And we were desperate. Gina and I needed time off so Pumpkin could have her operation. Our child couldn't wait any longer. Cooper was settled in. We'd decided he was at least competent and we had to leave him to cope as best he could.

'With both Gina and I away, the other doctors have been overworked so they've had little time to check that the nursing home was running satisfactorily. Then the charge sister here went off ill. If I'd been here I might have put one of the main hospital sisters across in a charge capacity—but that's easy to say in hindsight.

'Regardless, I'm being told from every quarter now I'm back that Cooper has to go—and, after hearing what Rob has to say of Cooper's reaction this morning, I agree.'

The medical director ran a hand wearily through his hair and Meg could suddenly see the strain of a doctor with too much responsibility, as well as the demands of a young family with an ill child.

Rob saw it too.

'Hey, Struan,' Rob said gently. The vet rose and gripped the medical director's arm. 'You're done in, mate.'

'I'm fine.' Struan took a deep breath. 'I'll see Cooper now and get rid of him—pay him off, if I need to. Then I'll come back and do a full round of each patient and see there aren't any more disasters waiting to happen.'

'On top of your own work,' Rob said. 'On a Sunday.'

'Yeah, well, I've had six weeks off.'

'While your four-year-old had open heart surgery and you coped with an anxious wife, a toddler plus a teenager as well. Great holiday,' Rob jeered. He stood by his friend and looked straight at Meg. 'Can't we help him?'

Can't *you* help him, the look said. Can't *you* help *us*?

'I can help today,' Meg said slowly, rising to her feet and facing the two men, 'but I'm not registered to work in Australia. Already I've done more today than I legally should.'

'You could do a round of the patients here and let

Struan know of any problems, though,' Rob suggested, and Meg nodded.

'Of course I can.' That much was easy, but somehow Meg knew that one morning's work wasn't all that was being asked of her.

It wasn't.

'It's not just that,' Struan said heavily. 'Thanks for your offer, Meg, but we have a long-term problem here. Gina's still unable to work full time—in fact, until Pumpkin's a good deal better she won't be able to work much at all—and it takes up to a month to organise a locum. So now you've ejected Cooper. . .'

'I didn't eject Cooper,' Meg protested. Despite her confusion, she managed to smile. 'You can blame Dr Daniels for that. I've never seen such a brutal ejector.'

'I've never ejected so brutally.' Rob's eyes twinkled. 'Or with so much satisfaction.' He hesitated and his smile faded. 'Meg, I know this isn't fair when you've come so far for a holiday—but how about working here for a month? It seems to me that you'll solve a few personal problems by staying here—and if you don't then we'll have Struan overworked and Gina coming back to work while Pumpkin still needs her.'

'But. . .' Meg's smile faded. She stared helplessly up at Rob. 'But. . .'

Her words faded. There was complete silence in the room as both men watched Meg's face.

'I can't, Rob,' Meg managed at last. 'I didn't come to Australia to work. There's. . .there's Eve to consider. . . And I'm not registered to work here. We don't have anywhere to stay and we're going home. . .'

'You're not supposed to be returning to England until the end of the month,' Rob told her firmly. 'What are you intending to do until then?'

'I'm. . .I'm not sure. Find a beach somewhere. . . Travel down the coast to Melbourne. . .'

'By the time you get to Melbourne it'll almost be winter,' Rob retorted. 'Melbourne in winter. . . Well, you might just as well be in London. And will you be enjoying yourself? I doubt it. You'll never be able to take your eyes from Eve. And there's also the small matter of Spud, Meg. What are you intending to do with your convalescent mutt while you gallivant round the country on holiday?'

'Rob, who on earth is Eve?' Struan Maitland was clearly lost as he turned from Rob to Meg and back to Rob again. Now he raised his voice to cut across Rob's persuasive tone. 'Rob, am I being stupid—or are you talking right over my head?'

'Eve's Meg's young cousin,' Rob told him. 'She's thirteen years old and suffering from anorexia nervosa. Badly.'

'Anorexia. . .' Struan's eyes flew straight to Rob's and his eyebrows rose three inches. 'And you're keeping the child out on your farm, Rob?'

'Yes.' Rob's voice was clipped and tight—and suddenly the tension Meg sensed in the man surfaced all over again.

'Is that wise?'

'It's nothing to do with you,' Rob told his friend bluntly. 'What is your business is that I'm offering you a doctor on a plate.'

'You're not offering me!' Meg's voice rose to practically a wail. 'I'm not sitting on any plate, waiting to be offered, Rob Daniels. This is my holiday and you've no right to hijack it.'

'I'm not hijacking.' Rob's smile was gentle and hypnotically appealing. 'I'm just suggesting.' He touched her hand in a placating gesture of comfort. 'Meg, listen. Eve's already eating. If she's allowed to stay at the farm—well, a month of Maggie's cooking while Eve takes responsibility for her dog and has the run of the farm and the beach—don't you think that could work better than any touring holiday could?'

'I don't know,' Meg started slowly, and Rob nodded.

'I don't know either,' he agreed. 'But it could. Granted?'

'Yes, but. . .'

'But what?' He took her hands and gripped them hard, pressing his point like a sledgehammer. 'How are you thinking of taking Spud on this holiday of yours, Meg? An injured dog, being carted from hotel to hotel. . . And, Meg, we need you here. A month. That's all Struan and I ask, Meg, and at the end of that time you can pack up your cousin and dog and take yourself right back to the London fog and your devoted fiancé. . .'

'Fiancé. . .' Struan's eyebrows hit his hairline again. 'I haven't heard of any fiancé. You're engaged, then, Meg?'

'Yes, I am,' Meg said with asperity. 'Though you wouldn't think so the way Dr Daniels. . .the way this. . .this. . .'

'Are you looking for a description?' Rob's smile deepened. 'How about weasel?' he grinned—and Meg glared and tried hard to maintain rage in the face of a sudden overwhelming urge to choke on laughter.

'O-OK,' she managed. 'You're right as usual, Dr Daniels. I couldn't have thought of a better description myself. Weasel. Ingratiating, sneaking, overbearing. . .'

'And they're just my good points.' Rob smiled down at her, his eyes sympathetic as well as laughter-filled. Meg tried frantically to maintain her glare, but those mesmeric eyes met her rage with a look as bland as cream.

And finally Meg's lips twitched. Meg's fury dissipated like a popped bubble. She choked on a helpless chuckle—and both men joined her.

She caught herself soon enough, of course. Reality has a way of never receding completely. Finally Meg pushed back laughter and sought for words to repel what this man—this weasel—was thrusting her into.

'Rob, I can't. . .' She turned then to Struan. 'Dr Maitland, this man is like a bulldozer, and you're being bulldozed as well as me. You don't know the first thing about me.'

'So, tell him about you,' Rob interrupted, and Meg managed to glare again.

'Shut up, Dr Daniels.'

'I will if you tell Struan about yourself.'

'Rob. . .' Meg rose then and took a threatening step toward him—and Rob threw up his hands in mock surrender.

'OK, OK. Don't hurt me, lady,' Rob pleaded in mock terror. 'Just tell the nice doctor where you were trained.'

He had her laughing again—the weasel!

'Maybe you should tell me where you were trained,' Struan asked, amidst laughter, and when Meg found control enough to tell him he whistled.

'There are no problems there, Dr Preston. Your credentials sound impeccable.'

'Look, you don't know the first thing about me.' Meg's smile faded. 'Dr Maitland, you need references. . .'

'I had references for Cooper,' Struan told her. 'I'm almost sure the last place that employed Cooper simply wrote good references to get rid of him.' He shook his head.

'Dr Preston, I've seen your anger—rage—on behalf of an old lady you haven't met before. If you can be concerned about a patient like that—well, with your training, that's all I need to know. I'd be delighted to have you on my staff for a month—or more if you can manage.'

'But I can't,' Meg stammered. 'I told you. I'm not even registered to practise in Australia.'

'We can organise that,' Struan responded. 'We've been

given remote status here, which means that if we can persuade suitably qualified people from overseas to come then we can get their registration through fast. If we can get a faxed copy of your English registration, work experience and proof of identity down to Melbourne tomorrow I'll have you registered by lunchtime.'

'Just like that?'

'Just like that,' Rob interjected. Rob Daniels's hand came out and took Meg's arm. 'See. . .I told you it'd be easy.'

'And where. . .?' Meg said icily. 'Where am I going to stay?'

'With me, of course,' Rob smiled. 'On my farm. That's where Eve wants to stay.'

'Rob, this is ridiculous.'

'It's not ridiculous at all.' Rob's hands came swiftly up to grip Meg's shoulders, swinging her to face him and ignoring Struan's presence as he commanded all her attention. His smile faded and his face held reassurance and compassion.

'It's not the least bit ridiculous, Meg. Your Eve needs time to get herself together and by doing this you'll give her a chance. All of us—Struan and I included—are here to help with Eve. All we ask is that for the next few weeks you help us too. Is that so ridiculous?'

'Yes. . . No. . .' Meg put a hand up to a spinning head. 'Look, Rob, what on earth will I tell Paul?' She was so confused that she was almost talking to herself.

'Paul?' Struan queried blankly, and Rob flashed him a sideways grin.

'Paul's Meg's fiancé. We don't have to consider him. He's safely in London and long may he stay there.'

'Rob!' Meg's eyes flashed fire and she started to pull away—but Rob's hands gripped more tightly.

'It's OK, Meg.' Rob smiled and there was just the faintest trace of uncertainty in his smile. 'I won't repeat

Eve's comments on your choice of fiancé. But he's half a world away; you're here, and you're needed. Struan needs you desperately. Eve needs you to stay here and Spud also needs you. How can you resist such demand, Dr Preston?'

'But. . .' Rob Daniels was altogether too close for comfort. Those caring eyes, with laughter still lurking deep in their depths, were looking straight down into hers—causing a sensation deep within that Meg had never felt before and wasn't the least sure she wanted to feel now. It made her feel like her world was spinning crazily out of control. Her plans were being tossed aside as if they were of no import.

'But what about you, Dr Daniels?' she managed. 'What you're saying is that you intend sharing your house with Eve and Spud and me for a full month.' She took a deep breath. 'You know what they say, Dr Daniels. Fish and visitors stink after three days. How are you going to put up with us for four long weeks?'

Rob didn't smile then. The laughter faded from his eyes and for a long moment he stood, holding Meg's shoulders and looking straight at her—for so long that when he finally spoke she knew his words for absolute truth.

'You won't stink, Dr Preston. Believe me, you won't stink. After a month. . . Well, I have grave doubts whether a month will be long enough for me to even think you smell.'

CHAPTER SEVEN

SOMEHOW Meg got rid of him.

Somehow Rob was shoved out the door and Struan and Meg were left to discuss business. At the end of their discussion, though, Meg knew enough from Struan to realise that she really was needed, and she definitely would be doing the hospital a real service by staying.

'If I'm here to work, I may as well get on with it,' she told Struan as he finished outlining dull details, such as terms and conditions—not quite so dull, though, as Meg realised the job's generous salary would make life a little easier when she finally went home. Taking care of Eve was an expensive business, and she was determined that Paul shouldn't foot her cousin's bills.

Paul would pay, Meg knew, and he'd do so graciously—but it was his graciousness that grated! Paul's condescending niceness was one part of Paul's personality to which Meg was having trouble growing accustomed.

This was her fiancé she was thinking about, she thought doubtfully as she and Struan emerged from the sister's station. Funny, Paul seemed to be drifting further and further away from her. Half a world away. . .

Rob was nowhere to be seen as she and Struan finished their meeting, and Meg certainly wasn't asking for his whereabouts. Indeed, she was grateful for time away from Rob Daniel's bulldozing presence.

Meg had promised Struan that she'd spend some time now reading through patients' records for the nursing home—a job which had to be done immediately in the light of Cooper's incompetence, but also a job which could be done without medical registration. Struan, Meg gathered, had only returned to Gundowring on Friday and he was snowed under with administrative work. Struan briefly introduced Meg to the staff and, with gratitude, left Meg to it.

This was work so very different from the work Meg was accustomed to. Meg's life in the casualty ward of St Mark's went from dull to frenetic and back to dull in a matter of minutes. Here there were long-term patients to be cared for.

Would she enjoy such work?

Meg had never really considered anything other than the casualty job she did now, but at the back of her mind she'd assumed that one day she must look at general practice rather than emergency trauma work. Here she was, then, looking at it sooner rather than later, thanks to one Rob Daniels.

He truly was a weasel! So why did he make her laugh? Why did he do such strange things to her heart?

Meg spent an hour in the office, carefully reading and rereading the notes on each patient. Finally she glanced at her watch. It was almost twelve. She still had no idea where Rob was but presumably he had work of his own to attend to and would return in due course. While she was waiting it wouldn't hurt to wander through the building and put faces to the names on these notes.

There was the sound of voices coming from a room at the end of the corridor. Meg made her way there, feeling absurdly self-conscious. She felt that she had no rights here—and yet she was now employed to be in charge of the place. What a transition!

So, here goes, she thought firmly. Let's meet your charges. She took a deep breath and opened the door.

The moment the door swung wide ten pairs of inquisitive eyes swivelled straight to Meg. Glasses were adjusted on elderly noses for a better view, and Meg was scrutinised from head to toe. Meg had never been more grateful that she was wearing a dress and had gone to some trouble with her make-up. The old eyes of the room's occupants told Meg that her soft print dress was approved of, as was the prettiness of the girl who was wearing it.

'Well,' an old lady exclaimed from the far side of the room. The group had been playing cards but their cards now lay untended. Word had obviously travelled fast and a new doctor seemed to beat a hand of cards! 'Isn't she lovely?'

'Shh, Hilda,' the old man beside her reproved. 'She'll hear you.'

'Don't matter if she does,' the said Hilda retorted. She shoved herself to her feet and tottered forward. 'Welcome to Gundowring, dear,' she greeted Meg. 'We're very, very pleased to meet you.'

There was no doubting the warmth of their welcome— though Meg was left with a lingering feeling that anyone was welcome after Geoff Cooper. She fielded questions as best she could, shot in a few of her own and finally backed to the door.

'I must go,' she told them. 'There are others I haven't met.'

'All the real oldies.' Hilda nodded. 'The ones stuck in their rooms. Though there's more of them now than there used to be. We don't seem to get better fast with that Dr Cooper looking after us.' The old lady brightened. 'But you're a tonic just to look at, my dear. You'll find your young man in Room Five with Frank and Ethel.'

'My young man,' Meg said blankly, and the smile on each old face widened.

'Young Doc Daniels,' one of the men hooted from the rear of the room. 'And don't tell us he's not your young man cos we've got eyes in our heads and you walked past this window not much more than an hour ago hand in hand with the fella. It's about time our Doc Daniels found himself a decent woman, and that's a fact.'

Old heads nodded agreement—but Hilda took pity on Meg's mounting colour and shook her head reprovingly at her friends.

'Don't you let us busybodies interfere, dear,' she smiled. 'We'll pretend we didn't notice, if you like— but the very best of luck to both of you is all I can say. He's a very special young man, our Dr Daniels. I've known him since he was a baby and, well, he deserves a darn sight better than life's meted out to him, our Dr Daniels, and you look just special enough to be exactly what he needs.'

Meg took a deep breath. Some things had to be sorted out right now if she was to stay in this hospital.

'Mrs Cuthbert, Dr Daniels is not my young man,' she managed. 'As it happens. . .' She held out her ring finger for them to inspect her sizeable diamond. 'As it happens, I'm engaged to a very nice man back in England and in a month I'm going home to be married. My stay here is temporary.'

Their combined smile slipped.

'Well!' the old man at the rear gasped. 'Well, I never! What does this fiancé of yours think of your traipsing round hand in hand with our Doc Daniels?'

What, indeed!

'He'd just better not hear about it,' Meg said grimly and then humour bubbled up just when she needed it most. 'And if I catch anyone writing letters to England I'll replace every card pack in the place with Happy Families,' she threatened them.

Upon which she took her exit just as fast as she decently could.

Room Five with Frank and Ethel. . .

Half of Meg didn't want to find Rob Daniels now.

With the old people actively matchmaking and her plans and composure in tatters, what Meg desperately needed was a few quiet hours to herself. Maybe a phone call to Paul would help—to remind her just where her plans for the future lay. This place. . . This place was like some kind of web holding her fast, with Rob Daniels lurking deep within its centre.

' "Come into my parlour," said the spider. . .'

'Honestly, Meg Preston,' she told herself crossly, 'you're getting things totally out of proportion. At the end of four weeks you'll go home with a happier Eve and one mended dog—but everything else will be the same. At least, I'll be the same. . .'

She opened the door to Room Five and found that she wasn't the same in the least.

Rob Daniels was there—and the man had the power to unsettle her just by looking up at her with those deep, smiling eyes that did such dangerous things to her heart.

'Dr Preston. . .' Rob's eyes welcomed her. He was seated in an armchair at the side of the room and it seemed that he'd been watching television, of all things! Now he rose and introduced Meg to the two other occupants of the room—an elderly lady in another chair and a man in the bed. 'Ethel and Frank Simpson, I'd like you to meet Dr Meg Preston. Dr Meg's the new medical superintendent of our nursing home.'

It gave Meg a shock to hear herself so described. She shot Rob a doubtful look and then turned to greet the Simpsons.

'I'm pleased to meet you both,' she said with a smile. 'I've already met your horse and her new baby. Mildred's gorgeous.'

'She is, isn't she?' Ethel agreed shyly. 'Dr Rob has been showing us his video of the birth. He said you filmed it all, my dear. We're so grateful. We never thought. . . Frank and I never thought Mildred could recover enough to foal. Mildred means so much to us.'

'I can see that.' Meg's eyes flew to the television where Mildred was nuzzling her newborn foal, courtesy of Meg's filming. Not bad at all, she thought critically. The film wavered a bit but at least the camera had been aimed in the right direction.

She flicked an uncertain glance at Rob. So, that's why Rob was watching television. Going over the birth, moment by moment, for an ageing couple to whom their horse meant everything.

This man was some vet!

'Well, we'll leave you to your baby now,' Rob told the Simpsons in his deep, lazy voice. 'You can rewind the video and watch it over and over again—and tell me what I did wrong.' His grin told Meg that he knew they'd do just that.

'You should come out and see the foal for yourself before long.' Meg frowned slightly as she thought back to the notes she had read on Frank Simpson. He'd been transferred two weeks ago from the hospital across to the nursing home under the direction of Dr Cooper— and there were questions unanswered in the notes Meg had read.

'Mr Simpson, you had pneumonia after a heavy cold,' she queried softly, feeling her way. 'Did Dr Cooper think you needed long-term care? Is that why he transferred you here?'

'Frank's not getting any better,' Ethel quavered, answering for her husband. 'He's so weak he can hardly stand. We're starting to think he'll be in here for ever, and maybe I'd better make some arrangements to live closer. I mean, if he's not going to get any better. . . Dr Cooper says sometimes after a bout of pneumonia there's not a complete recovery.'

'No.' Meg flashed an uncertain glance at Rob, but his look encouraged her. Go on, girl, Rob's look said. You're every bit as competent as Cooper if not more so. Don't trust Cooper's judgement here.

OK, she wouldn't. Meg took a deep breath.

'Mr Simpson, there's nothing in your notes about physiotherapy,' she said slowly. 'Have you been having any?'

'No.' The old man looked doubtfully at his wife. 'I haven't, have I, Ethel?'

'There's only been the lady from the mobile library visited him since he's been in,' Ethel volunteered. 'Even when he was in the main hospital. Except for Dr Cooper every few days—and for friends and family, of course.'

Dr Cooper every few days. . . A man acutely ill with pneumonia. . . A man who had been active until his illness. . .

'Does the hospital have a physiotherapist?' Meg queried, and by her side Rob nodded, his face darkening. Rob's face was fast reflecting Meg's anger.

'Yes,' he told her. 'Liz Moran is our local physiotherapist. She comes into the hospital when any doctor or the nursing staff request it.'

'Then why. . .?' Meg paused and closed her eyes. She couldn't go further without implying that Cooper was incompetent—but maybe she was past caring if Cooper's feelings were hurt. 'Mr Simpson, have you been out of bed much since your illness?'

'Only to the bathroom,' the old man quavered. 'The truth is, Doc, my legs have gone all wobbly, and they're getting worse. Doc Cooper's right when he says I couldn't cope at home.'

'Well, your legs will keep on getting more and more wobbly if you don't use them,' Meg said bluntly. 'There's an adage in health care—*Use It or Lose It*—and it's absolutely true. The best way to lose the function of your legs is to stay in bed.

'Mr Simpson, I'm afraid your nice quiet hospital stay

is at an end. If I can I'll organise a physiotherapist to visit you this afternoon—if not, then she'll be here first thing tomorrow. The powers that be in this hospital will put you top priority for physio or they'll find themselves another doctor for this unit.' She smiled.

'I might as well throw my weight around before they have me signing any contract. And, while I'm throwing my weight around, Mr Simpson, I want you out of bed now, jelly legs and all.' She eyed Rob with a speculative gleam. 'Dr Daniels, how do you feel about working instead of sitting round watching television?'

'Work. . .' Rob's eyebrows rose. 'Work! Me? You have to know that the mere word's anathema.'

'Just shut up and get round to the other side of the bed,' Meg told him sternly. She grinned at his stunned expression. Rob Daniels had been bulldozing her all morning. It wouldn't hurt Rob Daniels to cop a bit of bulldozing himself for a change.

'Are you going to help me, Dr Daniels?' she asked Rob sweetly. 'Or are you only good for television-watching?'

'I don't know whether I like dictatorial women,' Rob said thoughtfully, and Meg nodded.

'Fine by me,' she agreed sweetly. 'I don't want you to like me. I want you to work for me.'

So for the next half-hour—while Ethel twittered behind them like an anxious hen and the nurses looked on from the sidelines with faces that told Meg they knew Frank Simpson had been neglected and they were ashamed—Dr Meg Preston and Dr Rob Daniels, doctor and veterinary surgeon, walked Frank up and down the corridors, coaxing him, supporting him and even gently bullying him.

Once nudged from his television, Rob worked magic. He seemed to sense the old man's needs, and between silliness, laughter and understanding he had Frank Simpson doing more than Meg had hoped for.

Finally Frank's footsteps started to falter, no matter how encouraging they were, and Meg deemed he'd done enough.

'OK, that's thirty minutes of exercise,' she told him, as Rob helped the old man back into bed. 'You've done really, really well, Mr Simpson. Those legs are losing their wobbles almost as we watch, and the way to get your chest clear and healthy again is for you to start exercising enough to use your lungs.'

She turned to the nursing sister as Rob adjusted the bedclothes over the thin old legs. 'He needs lunch and a couple of hours' rest now, but I'd like Mr Simpson out of bed in a chair for an hour this afternoon—sitting outside in the sun, if you can arrange it. I want him to walk there by himself, if he can. He'll need a nurse at either side for support, but you're only to support him if necessary. Could you see it happens, please, Sister?'

'But. . .' The nurse hesitated.

'But what?' Meg's voice was grim and the nurse almost visibly swallowed. Meg, it seemed, was heading for a reputation as a termagant.

'We haven't enough staff,' the nurse said slowly. 'There's only Sister Arnold and me on—and if one of the other patients need us. . .'

'Then Mr Simpson will wait until you're ready,' Meg told her, her voice absolutely inflexible. 'But his needs are a priority and you're to see that his needs are met. His exercise is imperative if he's to go home.'

'But. . .isn't Mr Simpson a long-term patient?'

'He certainly isn't,' Meg snapped. 'He should never have been admitted here in the first place. Your first priority, Sister, is to make your ill patients healthy, and if that means that paperwork or tidy wards have to wait then so be it.'

She hesitated, thinking plans through until tomorrow. A glance at Rob showed only approval—and his approval gave her the courage she needed. 'Sister. . .you know I'm in charge now,' she said slowly. 'I think. . . Well, even if I'm only working here for four weeks, for these weeks I want things done well. Could you organise a staff meeting for nine tomorrow? At that meeting I want everyone here who can possibly be here—kitchen staff, gardeners, everyone.

'We have twenty patients who need care from everyone if we're to make their lives enjoyable—and by the end of four weeks I want to see more going on in this place on a Sunday morning than ten people playing cards and ten people lying in bed. Is that OK, Sister?'

'A staff meeting. . .' The nurse nodded doubtfully as though such a thing was totally foreign to her. 'I'll try to arrange it.'

'No, Sister,' Meg said gently. 'You *will* arrange it. Now.'

'Whew!'

Rob led Meg back out into the sunshine, a bemused look on his face. He helped Meg into the Land Rover and turned out of the hospital car park, still with the same stunned expression.

'Have I done something wrong?' Meg asked cautiously, eyeing him from the far side of the car. She had gone in too heavily with the nursing staff, she thought ruefully. They already thought she was a dragon. Maybe Rob thought it was crazy for a temporary medical superintendent to take such a stern stand.

'No way.' Rob shook his head as he concentrated on the road. A faint smile twitched the corners of his mouth upward. 'I'm just wondering what I've let Gundowring in for.'

'A dose of me?' Meg grinned. 'Maybe you and Struan should have asked for my references after all.'

'Struan said there was no need,' Rob grinned. 'And

he's right, of course. The more I see of you, Meg Preston, the more I think that there's absolutely no need at all.'

He glanced again at her—and the look in his eyes told her that Rob Daniels wasn't just talking of her medical competency.

They didn't go home.

Meg had expected Rob to turn the car back toward the farm, but they deviated onto a side road just out of the town. Meg frowned. This was a gravel track and they hadn't come into town this way.

'Where are we going?' she asked cautiously.

'You're being hijacked, lady,' Rob smiled. He motioned to the mobile phone on the seat between them. 'We can both be contacted if we're needed but, seeing you're starting work tomorrow, I thought we might decree today a holiday.'

'A holiday.' Meg stared. 'But Eve's expecting me home.'

'Not Eve,' Rob said blandly. 'She gave me your bathing costume when I told her I was taking you swimming after we'd visited the hospital.'

'Eve gave you my. . .' Meg's jaw dropped about a foot. 'Look, what is this?'

'It's obvious.' Rob shrugged and smiled. 'It's an abduction. I told you I couldn't be trusted. Usually it's after midnight when I'm at my devious best, but I'm prepared to make exceptions in times of need. And this is a time of need, if ever I saw one. A magnificent Sunday with no imperative work and a lovely lady by my side. . .'

'Dr Daniels. . .'

'Dr Preston. . .' Rob copied her intonation exactly, mocking her with his smile.

Meg took a deep breath. Those eyes weren't to be trusted one inch. If he thought he was taking her willingly. . .no way!

'Rob, I can't leave Eve by herself,' she said desperately. 'It isn't fair on the child. And. . .and what about Spud? Shouldn't you be checking him?'

'I've already checked him,' Rob said firmly. 'Contrary to your obvious suspicions, lady, I am not entirely a gentleman of leisure. While you were in conference with Dr Maitland I saw two patients of my own—two rather nice cows, as a matter of fact, with an infection that threatened to spread through the herd if it wasn't treated. I've treated the pair of them, gathered their collective appreciation and while I was in a working frame of mind I rang home.

'Maggie reports Spud is improving hourly and recommends we don't come home. She thinks while Eve sees herself solely in charge she's blooming—and I agree with her.'

'Yes, but. . .' Meg fought back the smile this man tried to make her produce as doubt assailed her. Rob Daniels making her smile was all very well—but he could so easily sidetrack her from her responsibilities. 'It's a long afternoon,' she managed. 'I can't leave Eve all that time.'

'And I'm saying it'll do Eve good to be left.' Rob hesitated. 'Meg, if you make yourself responsible for your cousin every minute she'll never learn to trust herself again. You must let go some time—and what better time than when Maggie's her gentle overseer?'

'Yes, but. . .'

'And she won't be bored,' Rob went on inexorably. 'I've arranged company.'

'Company?' Things were racing way faster than Meg could keep up with here. She felt as if the race was almost to the finish line and she hadn't left the starting blocks.

'Struan's teenage daughter, Lisa, is coming over to the farm to keep her company,' Rob told her, his sideways look telling Meg that he understood the confusion she was feeling. 'Actually, Lisa is Gina's and Struan's adopted daughter. She's fourteen years old and a nicer kid you could never meet. She's been through traumas of her own—she never knew her dad, and her mother died of cancer—but she's pulled through it just fine.

'Lisa comes out to my farm every weekend and rides my horses. I rang her this morning and told her about Eve. Lisa's promised to take Eve riding—and it's my bet the girls will get on famously.'

'But. . .' Meg shook her head, bewildered. 'How do you know if Eve rides? I don't. . .I don't think she does.' She stopped, biting her lip. That sounded as if she hardly knew her young cousin—but, indeed, it was the truth. By the time Meg had met Eve, the young girl was already ill and in no state to be thinking of riding.

'She does ride, as a matter of fact,' Rob said smugly. 'Well, well, Dr Preston. You're being pipped at the post all over the place. I asked Eve this morning if she rode and she went all wistful on me. She says she had a pony as a child but her parents sold it when they sent Eve to boarding school.' Rob's smug expression faded. 'They don't sound the sort of parents I'd want as a kid myself.'

'They were horrid,' Meg said savagely. 'Dreadful. And Eve's so nice. . .' She shook her head. 'But Rob. . . Dr Daniels. . .'

'Rob.'

'Rob, then,' Meg managed faintly. 'Look, I don't know how Eve will get on with a girl her own age. She's so self-conscious. She might hate it.'

'Then let's let time tell us whether she hates it or not, shall we?' Rob said gently. Before Meg could anticipate what he intended Rob's hand came down to close over hers—only for a brief, fleeting moment, but long enough for warmth to flood through Meg's whole body. It was a gesture of caring and compassion which touched Meg to the core. 'Meg, I have the phone with me so Maggie can ring if she's the least concerned. So, let's leave Eve to sort out her own life for one afternoon, shall we?' Rob said gently. 'And let's concentrate on more important issues.'

'L-like. . .?' Meg could hardly make herself speak. She swung her eyes to the road ahead—to the glistening ocean-filled horizon—but she didn't see one thing. All she saw was a panic-filled blur. 'Like what?'

'Like this extremely tempting lunch Maggie's packed for us,' Rob told her. 'Like how cold the surf is and how warm the sand is between our toes. And like finding out why the hell I feel you're a part of me I didn't know existed until yesterday afternoon.'

CHAPTER EIGHT

MAGGIE'S picnic lunch was delicious but Meg, still deeply unsettled, sat on the sand and said as little as possible. She concentrated fiercely on her food. In different circumstances the quiche and salad and sparkling wine would have warranted such attention. Here, if she hadn't been concentrating quite so hard on not taking the least notice of Rob Daniels, Meg would have been enthralled by her surroundings.

Rob had brought her to a wonderful place. It was a tiny sheltered cove at the end of a track across three or four rough paddocks. They must have crossed private property to reach it, Meg thought, as such a magic place wouldn't otherwise be deserted on a Sunday afternoon.

Here they had the whole place to themselves. The sun-baked sand was soft to touch. Low waves ran in and out on the gently sloping beach, breaking the turquoise mirror of water with their foam, and on either side of the cove a line of rocks—reaching out to sea—made this place their private sanctuary.

Which was the last thing Meg wanted. A private sanctuary with Rob Daniels. . .

She ate without tasting, alternately playing nervously with her quiche and fiddling with her wine until finally Rob reached over and took the glass from her nerveless fingers.

'Had enough?' he asked gently.

'Yes. Can we go home now, please?'

'No. We haven't had a swim.'

'I don't want a swim,' Meg snapped. This man thoroughly unnerved her. She took a deep breath. 'Dr

Daniels, I don't. . .I don't want to be here with you. I
never asked for this—and what gives you the right to
interfere with my life?'

'I didn't think I was interfering, so much as helping,'
Rob said softly, and watched her face.

'I. . .' Meg swallowed, digging her fingers into the
sand as though for support. She closed her eyes, trying
to sort out her own jumbled feelings. 'You have helped,'
she said slowly. 'With Spud, I mean—and, of course,
with accommodation. But. . .you can't know what's best
for Eve. I have to find solutions for my cousin my way.
Somehow. . .somehow you've talked us into staying here
a month but if you think you can control me. . . Well,
Dr Daniels. . .'

'I don't think I'm controlling you,' Rob told her. He
rose and stood, looking down at her. The bright sun
glinted on his red-brown hair and the sea breeze tousled
the coarse hair under his open-necked shirt. It was
as much as Meg could do not to stare. Not to become
mesmerised by this charismatic man. . .

He smiled down at her and the charisma became more
compelling as he held out a hand to help her to her feet.
'Meg, I'm not trying in any way to propel you on a
course you don't want. All I'm saying is that you should
look at what's available before judging.'

'Meaning?'

'Meaning I could be right about Eve,' he said gently.
'As I could be right. . .' His smile faded and he looked
at her with eyes that were uncertain. 'I could be right
about us.'

Meg had been halfway to lifting her hand to meet his.
Now she snatched it back, as if it burned.

'Dr Daniels, you're being ridiculous.' She rose then,
backing away from him so that they stood a couple of
metres apart. This place was so wild and open—yet for
all its openness Meg felt trapped. As if she were locked

in a confined place with this man and there was no escape.

'Why am I being ridiculous?' Rob asked mildly. He made no move to come near her, and Meg had an almost hysterical sense that his decision to stay still was a similar tactic to that he'd use with a frightened wild creature. He was watchful and compassionate and so careful. . .

But he intended to get what he wanted.

She was being stupid. Stupid! Rob Daniels was just a man, after all. Just a man.

'Rob, no matter how. . .no matter why you want to get to know me, I don't see the point,' Meg managed. 'I'm. . .I'm engaged to be married. I'm not in the market for any sort of new relationship.'

'Now, that's just it,' Rob said calmly. 'Until yesterday—even until this morning—I would have said exactly the same.' He dug his hands deep in his pockets and his eyes narrowed as if he were trying to see past the glare of the sun. 'Until yesterday I thought I was destined to stay single. I didn't think. . .I didn't think I had anything left to give.'

Anything left to give. . . Despite her confusion, Meg felt her heart stir at the note of desolation in Rob's voice. Here were these shadows again—and part of her wanted to know so much. . .

'Then yesterday you drove in to my farm and I felt my whole foundation shift,' Rob continued. 'I looked at you and I thought—there is something. Some way I can give back. . . Some way I can care. . .'

'Rob, this is ridiculous,' Meg whispered. She hardly knew what he was talking of. Some past hurt. . . Some hurt that loving her could heal?

She wasn't available for loving. Not Meg Preston, happily engaged to an English surgeon and with her life mapped out before her. 'You've known me for less than twenty-four hours, for heaven's sake,' she whispered.

'What basis is that for. . .for caring?'

'I haven't a clue,' Rob said honestly. 'You're right, Meg. I may well be being ridiculous. But I know. . .I see in your eyes that what I'm feeling isn't entirely one-sided, and I'm saying that maybe we should give it a chance. Relax—and see where it takes us.'

'Straight to passion, I expect,' Meg managed bluntly. 'I've seen where that leads.' She shrugged. 'We deal with the consequences all the time in our clinics for unsupported single mothers. Sometimes we see them brought into Casualty as attempted suicides—or worse.

'Rob, my own mother had a dreadful time because she fell in love with my father. He was already married but they found passion, and passion was followed by years of regret. No, thank you, Rob Daniels. I want no part in that.'

'You want no part in passion?' Rob asked mildly. 'Is that why you're engaged to Paul?'

'That's none of your business.'

'It shouldn't be,' Rob agreed. 'Yet somehow it is, and why it is I don't think either of us can explain.' He spread his hands. 'Meg, you're not fifteen,' he continued slowly. 'I'm not offering a path to a home for women of ill repute—or even to a mortuary slab. Good grief, woman, that's ridiculous. . .'

Meg flushed crimson. Rob was right—damn him. She was being ridiculous. But she didn't want passion!

She was engaged to Paul—solid, sensible Paul, whose career matched hers and who was stable and safe and. . .

And passionless.

Paul was all the things Meg's mother had longed for and had wanted Meg so badly to find. Paul was secure. Safe. Predictable. All the things this man in front of her wasn't. Rob Daniels was a man with a past. A man haunted by shadows she knew nothing of. A man who was taunting her with a desire she had never felt before and which frightened the daylights out of her. A desire she had no way of dealing with.

And Rob saw naked fear flash across Meg's face, and his eyes softened.

'Hey, Meg, don't look like that,' he said gently. 'I'm not about to rape or ravish you—or even seduce you away from your estimable Paul. If you like, we will go home.' He smiled at her with an attempt to reassure her but all his smile did was frighten Meg more—because her body reacted to that smile in such a way that she veered straight to blind panic.

'All I ask is that we have a swim first, Meg,' Rob continued. 'I'm darned if I'll admit to Maggie that she made such a lunch on such a day and then we wasted it by going straight home.' He smiled again. 'Now, I'm going behind the rocks to put my bathers on—note, I'm being incredibly modest—and I won't appear again for ten minutes, to give you a chance to be the same. And then, Dr Preston, it's a big ocean and I swear we'll swim ten yards apart—I won't even splash in your direction. And then, after we've swum our fill, I'll take you chastely home. OK?'

It wasn't OK at all. Meg's ordered world was in tatters around her. Common sense resembled the fine grains of sand between her toes—a texture she just knew would slide away from her, no matter how hard she grasped.

Paul. . . She was engaged to Paul, for heaven's sake. Where was Paul when she needed him most?

'He's back in London,' Rob said, and Meg gasped. This man was a mind-reader, as well as everything else. An arrogant. . .an arrogant weasel! A caring, compassionate vet. And now a seer.

'I'm sure your Paul is a buffer against the world, Meg,' Rob continued gently. 'But you shouldn't have left him back home if you need a buffer. Here. . . Here you have to build your own defences—if you can.'

And he turned his back on her and strode off toward
the rocks to change.

Somehow Meg managed to put on her bathing costume—acutely aware of Rob's presence even though, as
promised, he was well distant and out of sight.

She shouldn't swim, she told herself, but not to swim
would be petty. Not to swim would be to admit that Rob
was right—that she was afraid. That she did need Paul
as a buffer and that she couldn't build her own defences.

She could. She would.

She just didn't know how.

Meg slid her costume over her slim body and a tiny
part of her—she swore it was only tiny—rejoiced that
the costume was new. It was a white one-piece, high cut
over her thighs and low cut on her breasts—and very,
very flattering.

Ridiculous to think such a thing. She should be swimming in neck-to-knee sackcloth, she told herself savagely.
She certainly shouldn't be aware of the effect she was
having on this infuriating stranger. This man she
hardly knew.

Once changed, she closed her eyes for one long
moment, letting the sun bathe her face in its comforting
warmth. Searching for sanity somewhere in the darkness.

This was only a swim, for heaven's sake. Only a
swim. . .

So go into the water and get it over with!

Despite Rob's disconcerting presence, after a while Meg
finally started to relax enough to almost enjoy herself.

The water was brilliant. It was so clear that Meg could
see her toes deep on the sandy bottom, yet the turquoise
water flashed around her in a million sparkling crystals.
Gentle waves caught her body and rolled her, and Meg
dived deep through their foam and tried to let her confused mind have some rest.

She hardly knew where Rob was. As he'd promised, he didn't approach her, seemingly content for them to swim far apart. Despite the distance, though, she was aware of him being in the water and the sense of his presence became almost overwhelming. This man didn't have to be near to be close. He only had to be within sight.

Or maybe not. Maybe he was close anyway—in a way Meg couldn't begin to understand.

She was being stupid.

She turned angrily away from the waves and swam out to where the water was just starting to swell. Here she floated on her back, letting the warm water caress her body as her confused mind searched for peace.

There were fish everywhere. In this sheltered cove the small fish obviously felt safe to feed. Even as Meg lay floating on her back she was aware of flashes of silver; darting past her fingers and brushing against her legs. The fish seemed to have no fear—and their courage was a lesson Meg stood in need of.

'Would you like to feed them?'

Rob's voice roused her from her reverie. As promised, he was still ten yards away. His long, lithe body trod water with ease as he held a small bag above the water. 'Permission to approach?'

'You. . .' Meg gulped and almost went under. What was she to say? You promised to keep right away from me?

She couldn't. The words sounded ridiculous, even in her head. How much more ridiculous would they have sounded out loud?

'You're. . .you're going to feed the fish?' she asked breathlessly, and Rob took her answer for agreement. The man swam like a fish himself, his sun-bronzed frame knifing through the water with the skill of one born to the sea. Three strong strokes and Rob was beside her. His broad, strong shoulder touched Meg's, sending a ripple of sensation down through her body.

Then, before she could draw away, Rob placed his hand in his bag and was scattering sodden breadcrumbs across the water.

The water erupted before them. Thousands of shimmering whiting went into a feeding frenzy as they fought for the bread. They were leaping high out of the water in numbers so vast that the water round the two swimmers resembled nothing so much as a glittering, wonderful whirlpool.

Despite her confusion and the tension all around her, Meg found herself laughing in delight. She looked out over the shimmering mass and, almost before she was aware of what he was doing, Rob took her hand and guided her fingers into the bag of sodden bread.

'Feed them yourself,' he smiled—and Meg did, crumbling the bread and watching the results with enthralled enjoyment.

'Now dive and feed them,' Rob ordered. Meg cast him a doubtful glance but Rob was offering her the open bread-bag almost absently, his face as absorbed as hers in the wonder of the moment.

Meg hesitated for one instant—but only for one. This was a place of miracles. The sun was warm on her face. The water was alive with beauty all around her, and Meg's body was vibrant with the sensation of the moment. She had never felt so alive. No matter how this man unsettled her, this moment would stay with her for ever—to be remembered with longing when she was back where she belonged. Back in London.

Back with Paul. . .

Drat Paul. Decisively, Meg shoved her hand in the bag again, and dived.

If, on the surface of the water, Meg had thought there were thousands of fish, underneath the surface there seemed to be tens of thousands. Despite not wearing goggles, Meg's eyes opened wide in sheer stupefaction. The fish were taking the bread right from her hand— small, trusting flashes of silver native fish treating Meg as a benefactor who was here for their enjoyment.

And beneath them all was a huge rock-cod, his vast form ponderously sliding up toward the slim, lithe bread-giver to accept his due. Meg almost laughed aloud as the silver flashes parted before him—like children standing back to let a respected elder take his share. She held out her hand to the old man of the sea and her offering was graciously accepted—and then the old gentleman backed off unhurriedly and left the children to their fun.

She had to have some air. Meg's lungs were bursting. She looked for one last time and then burst to the surface, her first breath a ripple of entranced laughter.

'Oh, how magic. . . What a magic place. . .'

'It is, isn't it?' Rob smiled. He'd been treading water, leaving her to enjoy her time below by herself. Now he watched her with her aspect of a benevolent genie, providing a treat for his protégé. 'That's my friend, Sam, you met under the water. He's been here since I was a child. I take every chance I can to come here.'

'I don't blame you.' Meg smiled at him, the first genuine smile of pleasure and ease that she'd shared with this man. 'Have we any bread left?'

'It's all gone,' Rob said dolefully. 'They've eaten a whole loaf. These guys cost me a fortune.'

'You buy it especially for them?'

'Maggie gives me a really hard time,' Rob smiled. 'Every week she does the grocery list and every week I add bread for the fish, sugar lumps for all my recalcitrant horse patients—and one feed-the-masses-sized block of chocolate.'

Meg couldn't help smiling right back at him. 'So, who's the chocolate for?' she asked, and Rob grinned.

'For my very favourite patient,' he told her solemnly. 'Me! I prescribe it every time my stress levels rise—and you'd be amazed how often that happens. Sometimes it's three squares after every meal and sometimes—well, often it's the whole block.'

'I don't believe you,' Meg smiled, her eyes running over Rob's muscular body. There wasn't an ounce of extra fat on his spare frame. Her eyes dropped to the water where Rob's chest gleamed wet and bare—and then Meg flushed crimson as she caught herself following the lean line of his chest down to the hollow flatness of his belly. What on earth was she thinking of?

An image of Paul's out-of-condition body was super-imposing itself on Rob's—and Meg didn't like the comparison one bit.

She bit her lip, avoided Rob's perceptive eyes and turned resolutely to face the shore.

'We'd better go,' she said shortly. 'Eve. . .I don't want to leave her any longer.' She took a deep breath, glanced behind her to wait for the next wave and caught the surge neatly, letting its power hurl her toward shore.

Rob caught the same wave. The man was quicksilver fast, and he was much stronger in the water than she. Together they surfed toward the shore, the power of the wave holding them together as it rolled them on.

Meg was so acutely aware of his presence. She couldn't escape from it. It was as if Rob Daniels were somewhere inside her head and it'd take more than surgery to remove him. He was with her. . .as one with her. . .

The sensation was crazy.

Finally the wave dumped them both in the shallows. Meg surfaced to find Rob already on his feet, his hand reaching to steady her—to pull her up beside him.

'Rob. . .' Meg made a futile attempt to pull away but it was just that. Futile. Some force was coming in to play here that was beyond her. Meg could no sooner find the strength to pull away than she could have flown.

'Meg, don't go. . .' Rob's voice was an order but there was an overtone of tenderness that caught Meg on the raw. His two hands held hers, a strong warm link between two wet bodies. He smiled down at her, his eyes a trace uncertain. Then he glanced out toward the horizon, his face changed and he motioned Meg to look outward as well.

'See, Meg.' His voice was a whisper, almost as if he was talking to himself. 'The sea mist is coming in. It's a natural occurrence here—a soft warm mist caused by mountains meeting sea. The locals love it and so do I. I figure it's why I finally came back. Sea-mist healing, they call it. It stops the worst of the heat in summer and it seems to stop the cold in winter. This place has a reputation for healing and it's all because of the sea mist. Stay for a minute, Meg. Let the sea mist come in—and see what it can do for both of us.'

'It's not me that needs healing,' Meg said helplessly. 'Eve maybe, but not me. I don't. . .'

'But I do, Meg,' Rob said, and his voice was suddenly full of fatigue. 'I do. You don't know how much. And holding you. . . Holding you while the sea mist rolls in around us is just. . .it's just what I need most in the whole world. What I need most is right here in my hands. It's all around me and I'd be a fool if I let it slip away. It heals. . .'

'Even. . .even more than a slab of chocolate?' Meg whispered gently, striving for lightness as she looked up into Rob's strangely troubled eyes. There were so many things about this man that Meg didn't understand. All she knew. . .all she knew was that now suddenly Rob was asking her to help him—and she was powerless to resist. Not while these hands held hers and the force between them grew stronger with every minute.

'Even more than chocolate,' Rob murmured. 'Even more than sea mist.' He was looking straight back down at Meg now. His hands were pulling her against him so that their wet bodies touched; his hard, bare chest pressed against the soft compliance of her breasts. 'You, my lovely Meg. You can feel it too. You can feel that you have the power. . .'

No, Meg's mind was screaming. No. . .

But her eyes were locked to Rob's, her face turned up to his and the power he talked of was absolute. Meg was utterly incapable of resisting, and when Rob lowered his face to kiss hers Meg's lips tilted upward as if to find her home.

To kiss Rob. . .

It was the sweetest kiss she had ever known. At twenty-eight Meg was hardly inexperienced but this. . . Here was something Meg had never experienced in her life before as her whole being responded to Rob's touch.

It was as if their bodies were melting, one into the other, in a moment so indescribably sweet that Meg felt she was soaring. . .

Loving. . . Opening her heart to a feeling she had never dreamed could exist.

She felt her lips open to welcome him and deep within she felt her heart unfurl like a rose that had stayed in bud far too long.

The soft waves ran round Meg's legs in a caress of their own. Rob's hands fell to her waist, pulling her yielding body into the curve of his hard frame—and the kiss deepened and deepened as if it would never end.

Neither wished to end it. Meg's lips parted as Rob's tongue gently penetrated—searching, exploring, tasting until Meg's body was on fire with the glory of the moment. She had never felt like this. She hadn't known that her body could respond so fiercely. She hadn't known that such sweetness could exist. Her hands fell of their own accord, running down Rob's broad back and holding him closer. . .closer. . .

And then somehow they were slipping down into the shallows—to where the water ran in and out and they could lie full-length against each other on the wet sand, glorying in their nearness and deepening their kiss until Meg felt she was drowning in a joy so great. . .

So great. . .

She was laughing and sobbing and loving, and yet she was motionless, caught to Rob's being with a force that held as if she would never be released. Her hair was wet and streaming back over the sand. The water was washing in round her body and Rob was above her, his hands under the wet sand holding her and his mouth intent on knowing her completely.

Completely. . .

There was no completeness in this union. There couldn't be. Not with so many unanswered questions.

But there was joy. . .

And then a wave bigger than the rest smashed over them, submerging the entwined couple completely. It broke them apart as nothing else could have, and man and woman were forced to fight for breath.

And Meg found herself kneeling in the surf, part laughing, part choking—and all of her frightened near out of her wits.

Reality slammed home with a vengeance.

Dear heaven, this wasn't Paul. This man wasn't part of Meg's safe future, so carefully planned to avoid the mistakes of her mother.

This was a man she didn't know—who lived half a world from her security. This was a man of shadows of whom Meg knew nothing, a man of shadows making love to her as if she were his tomorrow.

Meg's tomorrow was England. Meg's tomorrow was Paul.

And Rob... The wave had broken them apart completely. Rob knelt, watching Meg across the foaming water, and the look in his eyes reflected her own confusion.

Something had happened... Something had happened in the last few moments that Rob hadn't expected. He'd wanted his sea-mist healing but he'd gained more than that. More than healing. Rob's eyes told Meg that he'd discovered an emotion so strong that it was threatening to destroy them both, and his eyes also told her that he was backing off as if burned.

Meg stared out over the shallows at Rob and what she saw confused her utterly. He'd wanted to kiss her. He'd wanted her, Meg's heart screamed. So, why was he reacting like this? It wasn't making sense at all.

This was madness. Meg hadn't wanted this man to kiss her, but as she knelt in the shallows and watched Rob's look of denial and rejection her heart made a huge discovery. She hadn't wanted Rob Daniels to touch her—yet she was willing him now to reach for her again. To sweep her doubts aside and take her again in his arms.

And the look on his face said that it wasn't going to happen.

She had to make the first move. She must.

She had to be sensible.

Meg closed her eyes, letting her hands drift helplessly down through the water. 'Please, Rob...I need to go home.'

'I guess. I guess maybe we both do.' Rob's voice sounded shaken to the core. He let his breath out and Meg saw his shoulders sag. A look crossed his face that could almost have been taken as defeat—of resignation to a lifetime of loneliness.

And something else. The impression of fatigue deepened—a fatigue not caused by sleepless nights but something else so deep that Meg couldn't touch it.

What? Why?

It didn't matter. It couldn't be allowed to matter. Rob Daniels' shadows could be nothing to do with an English girl happily engaged to a man on the other side of the world. Could they?

Meg rose shakily to her feet, stumbling to find her footing in the soft sand, and for once Rob made no attempt to help her.

'I'll get dressed,' she said unsteadily—and Rob nodded and turned away.

It seemed that Rob had come to a decision, and Meg wondered if it had been the wave that had broken them apart—or if it had been the realisation that there were emotions at play here that were stronger than both of them. And maybe. . . The look on Rob's face said that maybe Rob wanted those emotions to run out of control even less than Meg herself did.

CHAPTER NINE

MEG was almost decent when the phone rang.

Rob's mobile phone was in the picnic basket, and he was still over the headland, dressing, when its ring broke the stillness. Meg glanced uncertainly in Rob's direction. There was no sign of him. She had no choice but to answer it.

It was no ordinary phone call.

'Please. . . Is that Dr Daniels?' a voice whispered on the other end of the line.

It was a child speaking—and by the sound of the whispered question it was a very young and a very frightened child at that.

Meg's confusion and her attempts to button her dress and hold the phone at the same time were forgotten.

'This is Dr Preston,' Meg said, responding immediately to the fear in the child's tone. Nothing else was important. With fear like this it would have been stupid to make the child wait while she called Rob. Instead, Meg tried her most reassuring voice. 'I'm helping Dr Daniels,' she told the terrified child at the other end of the line. 'Will you tell me what the problem is?'

'Please. . .' The child seemed to be fighting for breath through sheer terror. 'Please. . . A dog's killed my hens.'

'A dog's killed your hens.'

Meg winced as her mind raced. Memories of the farmer's roadside story of Spud's attacks on his poultry flooded back. Could Spud have. . .?

He couldn't. The fear in the child's voice wasn't of an event that had happened days ago. The fear was for now.

'Oh, dear. Has he killed them all?' Meg asked, softening her tone to sympathy now that the child had decided to confide in her. The child sounded no more than eight or nine years old—maybe even younger.

Meg's sympathetic tone, though, disguised her racing thoughts. Surely it should be an adult calling Rob for help, rather than this terrified child?

'He's killed most of them,' the child quavered. 'He's killed Ruby and Chucky and Cleo and. . .and Peggy. And I ran out to stop him killing more and I hit him with my hand. And then he bit me and he bit me again. He. . .he killed Rhonda anyway and Mary's flown up a tree and she's bleeding and my arm's all bloody too. . . And. . .'

The child's voice faded. Terror was still there—but also a strange lethargy that started alarm bells ringing in the back of Meg's head. Alarm bells which were almost deafening.

'So your mum asked you to call the vet?' Meg asked carefully. Every fibre of Meg's consciousness was tuned into the situation now. She was vaguely aware of Rob approaching along the beach, but she turned her back on him to give the child her total, undivided attention.

'My mum. . . My mum's not home.'

'Is any grown-up home with you?' Meg asked, and grimaced as the child hiccuped on a frightened sob.

'N-no. Mum and Dad are down the bottom paddock.'

'I see.'

Rob had reached Meg now. She sensed him behind her and turned to put up a hand to ward off questions. Rob took Meg's cue on the instant, his eyes sharpening into concentration as Meg kept speaking. 'Sweetheart, is the dog. . .? Is the dog near you now?'

'N-no. It's outside and the door's shut. I want to find Mum and Dad, only I need to go past the dog but it bit me until I came inside. I think. . .I think if I go outside it might bite me again. And Dr Daniels's number was written by the telephone.'

The weariness was intensifying—as if it was all just too hard. Meg's hand whitened with tension as she gripped the telephone.

'So you thought you'd stay inside and ring for help,' Meg said, only the slightest tremor in her voice revealing her anxiety. How badly had the child been bitten? If shock took over. . . If the child lost consciousness before telling Meg where she was. . . 'You're very, very clever to phone the vet so quickly,' she said firmly, trying hard to make her voice sound normal. 'Sweetheart, tell me your name and where you live, and Dr Daniels and I will come to help you.'

Silence.

'Tell me your name, little one,' Meg ordered sharply, raising her voice school-marm style. Please, God, let the child not have lost consciousness. . .

'My. . .my name's Holly Edwards,' the child quavered and Meg breathed again. 'And. . .and we live on Morrisons Road in a white house. But. . .' Her voice trailed off. 'I. . . My arm. . . There's blood spurting out and I feel all funny. I want my mum but I'm not game. . .'

'Holly, you're not to try and find your mum.' Meg's fear had communicated itself to Rob. The connection was excellent and the child's fearful voice reached Rob almost as clearly as it reached Meg. He'd heard enough to sum up the situation and, with his eyes still on Meg, he was hauling their belongings into the basket as he listened. 'You mustn't go anywhere near the dog, Holly. You keep that door shut tight. Holly, is there a towel or dry dishcloth near the phone?'

'Y-yes.'

'And do you have a sofa somewhere near? Something comfy to lie on?'

'Yes.'

'Well, Holly, as soon as you put down the phone I want you to wrap the towel or dishcloth round your arm to cover the bleeding. Wrap it just as tight as you can and press on the bleeding part. Then I want you to lie with your arm lifted in the air or, if it hurts too much, prop it up high on cushions or on the back of the sofa. It won't hurt more than it does now and if your arm's up in the air it'll make the bleeding slow down.

'Then lie really, really still and tell yourself how brave you are until we come. Listen for our car. We'll be there in minutes, Holly, I promise. Your mum and dad might come home first, but we're coming anyway. OK, Holly?'

'O-OK.'

'You're a very sensible, brave girl,' Meg said strongly. She took a deep breath and glanced at Rob. 'Dr Daniels is here with me now, Holly. Dr Daniels, do you know where Holly Edwards lives—on Morrisons Road?'

'Yes.' Rob was wasting no words.

'OK, then, Holly. You heard. Dr Daniels knows just where you live, and we're coming. You see if you can stop the bleeding before the first grown-up arrives. And, Holly, you're not to go near the door to outside. Promise?'

'I. . .I promise.'

'Brave girl. Hold on, Holly. We're on our way.'

'It'll take ten minutes to get there.'

Almost before Meg rang off Rob was striding up the beach, with Meg following as best she could. He'd clearly heard enough to assess the situation almost fully. 'There's no one closer than us,' he snapped, thinking aloud as he moved. 'The other farm down that road is run by a hopeless old derelict. There's no way he'll get there before us, even if we can get him to answer the phone. How bad is it, Meg?'

'It sounds like the blood's pumping. Maybe there's a torn artery. . .' It was all Meg could do to talk. Her feet were flying and she was fighting for breath. 'But surely the child's parents will be back in that time.' Swiftly she filled in Rob's missing gaps and he winced without slowing at all.

'Stupid fools. Anna and Richard Edwards are horse-mad. If there's a horse in trouble they'd put it before their daughter every time. To leave a little one in the house alone. . .'

'How old is she?' Meg asked fearfully.

'Five, maybe. Certainly not much older.' Rob threw the picnic basket into the back of the Land Rover with a force that propelled most of its contents back out over the tray. 'She just started school this year. Five years old and they treat her like an adult. Stupid, stupid fools.'

The violence in Rob's voice made Meg's eyes widen. Either Rob knew something that she didn't here—or there was something in this man's background that was making him react with this fury. The shadows again?

She couldn't think of shadows now. Meg was already in the Land Rover, holding onto her seat for dear life as Rob planted his foot on the accelerator and gunned his vehicle back along the rough track as if the dogs of hell were on his heels.

What lay between Meg and Rob—all their unanswered questions—was pushed aside. Unimportant for now. There was only the road ahead, and how to cover it in as little time as possible.

It didn't take ten minutes.

Rob drove the miles between the beach and the Edwards' farm like a man possessed, and by the time Holly's house came into view Meg had been jolted almost to a pulp. She was sure she'd left her stomach somewhere back near the beach. An ambulance ride had never been so hair-raising.

Somehow, following Rob's instructions, Meg managed to telephone the hospital on Rob's mobile phone as they drove. To her relief, the receptionist put her straight through to Struan Maitland.

'Maybe it's just a simple dog bite,' Meg told the medical director as she finished outlining the situation. 'But, Struan, by the sound of the child's voice, I doubt it. You know I don't have medical supplies. Could you send an ambulance with saline and plasma and morphine. . .?'

'We're on our way, Meg,' Struan said grimly. 'It's a good twenty minutes from here, though. Until then, you and Rob are on your own.'

They certainly were. Meg cast an uncertain glance across at Rob and bit her lip as a feeling of helplessness engulfed her.

Still. . . There were worse people to be with in an emergency than Rob Daniels. Much worse. Meg's unease at Rob's presence had dissipated. Right now, Meg Preston was blessedly glad that Dr Rob Daniels was by her side.

The house was on a rise, and a quarter of a mile before they reached it Rob's hand hit the horn. Three short blasts, three long and three short—SOS. Rob sounded it over and over again in those last few moments of driving.

'Anna and Richard should hear that across the paddocks and if they don't head for home they don't deserve a child,' Rob said savagely. 'And at least Holly will hear us coming.'

If Holly was still conscious, Meg thought grimly as they careered in through the farm gate and she silently mouthed the prayer she'd been saying over and over on this crazy drive. 'Please, God. . .'

And then she stopped as she saw what lay before them.

The farmyard was a scene of absolute carnage.

Holly's chickens had obviously been allowed to roam free. They were past enjoying their nomadic lifestyle now, though, and past it for ever. Littered across the yard

were pathetic mounds of bloodied chicken carcasses.
There were feathers everywhere—and near the back door
was a mangy black dog, ripping one of the dead bodies
to pieces.

As Meg tumbled from the car the dog took the carcass
solidly into its mouth, backed against the door-screen—
and growled.

Before Meg could move toward the door Rob was at
her side, his hand gripping her like a vice and pulling
her back.

'No, Meg. If we go this way we have it cornered.'

Meg stared—and then saw what Rob meant. There
was a long line of lattice on either side of the back porch.
The dog had obviously settled in a sheltered spot with
its kill. Once Meg and Rob reached the gate into the
house yard the dog could only get past by attacking.

'We must.'

'Not here. Round the other side. Run.'

Without hesitation, Rob grabbed Meg's hand and
hauled her past the rows of lattice and around to the
other side of the house. Here a four-foot fence divided
garden from paddocks.

'I'll climb first,' Rob said grimly, but Meg was already
climbing, clambering over the barbed wire as if it were
a ladder. There was no way that she was being left behind.
She landed on the other side before Rob, squashing a
bed of annuals in the process. She didn't notice. Rob
dropped beside her, and by the time Meg found her feet
he was at the big front door.

'Holly!' Rob's deep voice reverberated around the
garden and beyond. 'Holly, are you there? It's Dr
Daniels.'

There was no answer and the door was hugely, immov-
ably locked.

'It won't have been used in years,' Rob said grimly.
'Farms' front doors aren't. Hell. . .' Then he looked at

the object Meg was holding out to him. As she'd found
her feet in the flower-bed Meg had lifted an edging tile—
a heavy half-circle of ceramic. Thoroughly serviceable.

'Throw it through the window,' Meg said urgently.
'We *must* get in.'

Meg didn't need to go further. Rob took two fast strides
to where a window led inside to an empty hallway, raised
his hand, threw the tile and the glass shattered inwards.

By the window were roses on staunch supports. Rob
wrenched a pole free to clear the window-frame of broken
glass. In seconds he was inside the house.

For a moment Meg lost sight of him—then the front
door opened inwards and they were flying through the
house in search of one small girl. . .

They missed her in their first frantic run through the
house. Finally Meg reached the kitchen door and turned.
The child was crumpled on the sofa—a tiny, limp figure,
with blood oozing through a towel wrapped tightly round
her arm. A figure not much larger than the cushions
surrounding her. . .

She was unconscious.

'Rob,' Meg screamed, and flew to the child's side.

There was still a pulse. It was faint and fluttering but
still there.

The cloth wasn't tight enough. Holly had done her
best but her failing strength hadn't been enough to stop
the bleeding. As she'd lost consciousness she'd rolled
sideways, removing the pressure and letting her arm fall.
The instant she felt a pulse Meg was unwrapping the
wound, forming the blood-soaked towel into a wad
and shoving it hard into a pressure pad over the
gaping wound.

The child was so small. To lose this much blood. . .
The scene in the kitchen and living-room almost matched
the blood-bath outside.

The child was dying. . .

'Tell me what to do.' It was Rob, standing over Meg—his eyes calmly assessing the situation. The only major wound seemed to be on the child's arm and there was little he could do to assist Meg to stop the bleeding. His thoughts were racing, regardless. 'There's saline in the truck, Meg. It's vet quality but surely it must be OK?'

Yes! Meg needed blood or plasma as well, but saline at least would bulk the body's fluid loss until the ambulance arrived.

'Oh, yes. Go,' Meg breathed—but Rob was already running back out through the front door to the devastation beyond.

For the next few minutes Rob and Meg worked with a speed only possible when adrenalin was running high.

Rob was back in moments, and together they set up a drip. The syringes Rob used for his animals were probably not as stringently safeguarded as human syringes, but Rob was a careful vet and his animals would be treated as thoughtfully as any human patients. Meg therefore used his equipment with confidence.

They worked as one. Rob Daniels could so easily have been a doctor, Meg thought fleetingly as he anticipated her every need and provided swabs, dressing and syringes from his capacious bag, handing each to her before she asked. The intravenous lines, it seemed, were identical for animals and humans.

'And just as sterile,' Rob reassured Meg again, holding the tiny undamaged arm so that Meg could do her work. 'We have our standards. . .' Then he laid the little arm back on the settee as a shout sounded outside—and the faint sound of an approaching siren.

'Here's Holly's mum and dad, if I'm not mistaken,' Rob said grimly. 'And Struan. Meg, I'll have to deal with the dog. If they come barging in the back door we'll have someone else bitten. Are you right here?'

'Just get me the plasma as soon as the ambulance

arrives,' Meg said grimly. 'Please, Rob. . .'

'It's on its way.' He placed a fleeting hand against Meg's face, and he was gone.

Meg was left, cradling the tiny child against her. Between them, Meg and Rob had done all they could. Now. . . The injured child needed plasma but almost as badly Holly needed warmth and comfort. How terrifying to face what this little one had faced alone!

Shock was taking its toll. The little girl seemed so cold. She lay limply in Meg's arms, but her eyes flickered open momentarily.

'Hey, Holly,' Meg whispered as the shock-dulled eyes fluttered closed again. The child was drifting in and out of consciousness and who knew whether Meg could be heard? But it was better to talk than to stay silent. 'You're safe now,' Meg continued. 'I'm Dr Preston. I'm a people doctor so I'm here to look after you while Dr Daniels rescues your hens.'

There would be time enough later to tell the child that there were few hens left to rescue. For now, Meg had the satisfaction of seeing just a little of the shocked pallor ease from the child's face.

'I want my mummy,' Holly whispered in a thread of a voice so faint that Meg had to stoop low to hear.

'She's on her way,' Meg promised. 'It takes a while to walk up through the paddocks.'

She was here already. Meg could hear a woman's voice outside, raised in terror and protest. The woman was obviously being barred from the back entrance. Rob's voice cut across the protests—then they were drowned out by the siren, louder now. Tyres squealed and the siren cut off sharply as the ambulance pulled into the yard.

Meg held Holly close, cradling her tightly and murmuring meaningless reassurances as the noises outside changed. There were more voices—Struan's, Meg thought, and that of an unknown male. A moment's silence followed, then a single low yelp and Rob's low voice, murmuring instructions.

A minute—another—and then the back door burst open and all the world seemed to tumble into the house.

Struan was there and an ambulance driver and Holly's parents, who were nearly hysterical with shock and disbelief. Following them was an old man, stinking of cow dung and booze and yelling that the kid must have teased the bloody dog and it wasn't his fault. . .

And Rob.

Somehow Rob was ignoring everything as he cleared a path through to Meg with the precious plasma. Then, as Struan and Meg moved into overdrive with their vital equipment and supplies, Rob somehow turned pandemonium into order.

He moved a chair so that the weeping mother could sit beside Holly as Meg and Struan worked—and somehow he persuaded the woman that she must be calm. Somehow his persuasion worked so that Holly's mother seemed almost sensible and didn't frighten her daughter further.

Not so simple was Rob's job of hauling the distraught father from the stinking old man. By the look of it the father had murder on his mind. Somehow, though, Rob hauled them both outside to whatever chaos was out there.

Rob Daniels. . . A man for emergencies. A man who performed triage—the prioritising of needs in a crisis— as if disasters were an everyday part of his working life.

Struan Maitland was no one's fool either, and Meg sagged in gratitude as she realised that in Struan she had a doctor every bit as competent as the doctors she worked with back in London. Struan administered morphine almost as soon as he reached the child's side, and within moments the drug took effect. The little girl had her mother. The child had the help she'd called for. Holly's shocked little eyes closed again and she slumped into drug-induced sleep.

'She's not. . .she's not. . .?' the mother quavered.

'She's not unconscious,' Struan told the woman curtly. He looked at Meg, who had finished adjusting the drip. 'Ready to move her, Dr Preston? The sooner we get Holly to hospital the better.' He looked across at Holly's mother, and his expression softened a little. 'Will you come with Holly in the ambulance, Mrs Edwards?'

'Yes. . . Oh, yes. . .'

'Ready,' Meg murmured, and the ambulance driver moved to replace Meg by Holly's side. In minutes the child was settled in the ambulance, the driver was at the wheel and Struan was holding the door wide. Meg followed the stretcher out into the yard, and as soon as she emerged Rob was by her side. The argument between Holly's father and the old man was continuing at full volume, but it was clearly all noise and posed little threat to either.

'Meg, I'd like you to come with us,' Struan said briefly. 'The little one knows you now and it'll give her some continuity if you stay with her in Theatre.'

Meg nodded. She knew as well as Struan that the immediate danger to the child would be shock. It could kill faster than anything else.

'OK.' She looked uncertainly at Rob, and he placed a reassuring hand on her shoulder.

'I'll collect you at the hospital,' Rob said briefly, and his hand came down to touch hers in a fleeting gesture of comfort—a gesture that went straight to Meg's heart and stayed there. 'I'll be there in about an hour.' He looked grimly round the yard. 'I need to stop these two from killing each other—but there's more work to be done here besides peace-making.'

There was, indeed. Meg looked swiftly round the

bloody farmyard and shuddered. She looked up at Rob—
and his eyes gave her the same message that his touch
had done.

Warmth flooded right through Meg's entire body.

This was crazy. Crazy, crazy crazy.

Crazy or not, it took a huge physical effort for Meg
to turn away—to step into the ambulance, have the doors
close behind her and be driven away from the man Meg
was beginning to feel was a part of her very being.

CHAPTER TEN

BY THE time Rob arrived at the hospital to collect Meg Holly had decided to live, and the medical team of Gundowring had made sure that she would have as few scars as possible.

It had taken more than an hour to stitch the child's tiny arm, and during that hour Meg had seen Gundowring's medicos at their best. The hospital had a highly competent surgical team—Lloyd and Sally were husband-wife team as well as anaesthetist-surgeon, Meg gathered, and this country district was certainly lucky to have them.

At Struan's request, Meg stayed in Theatre until Holly was deeply unconscious under anaesthetic—and then stayed on to assist. She watched with fascination as Sally's nimble surgeon's fingers carefully repaired a torn artery and damaged nerves, giving the little girl a good chance of recovering the full use of her arm.

Gina—Struan's wife—appeared halfway through the operation. Gina, Meg learned, was the hospital's paediatrician, and with Gina's presence the child had an operating team that had to be the equal of any in a city hospital. It was impressive indeed—and as Meg listened to the friendly cross-chat between the team and watched their mutual concern for their tiny patient she had an almost overwhelming desire to be part of it.

Which she was. For a month.

Only for a month! Why did the thought of such a restricted time suddenly seem so bleak?

Finally the arm was dressed, the anaesthetic reversed and the team relaxed.

'She'll do,' Sally said, satisfied. The young surgeon turned to Meg as she pulled off her gloves. 'Thanks to you, Meg Preston. You did a fine job to keep her alive. If you hadn't persuaded Holly to wrap her arm before you reached her. . .'

She fell silent.

She didn't need to say more. Holly had nearly died, as it was. If she'd lost even more blood. . .

'Well, it was also thanks to Rob Daniels,' Meg smiled, shaking off the nightmare of what could have been. 'I just hope the saline infusion is the same for humans as it is for dogs.'

'It's done the trick here,' Sally said warmly. 'I guess if Holly starts barking and develops a taste for Meaty Bites her parents might sue—but for now they should be darned grateful they had Rob's medical kit available.' The surgeon looked down at the tiny girl's pale face. 'In fact, they should be darned grateful they still have a daughter.' She sighed. 'Fools that they are. I can imagine Rob must be pretty upset.'

'He is,' Meg said slowly. She frowned as their little patient was wheeled out to Recovery. 'Sally, am I imagining it, or is there some reason for you to say that—for Rob especially to be so upset?'

The surgeon paused, and Meg was sure that she sensed inner shutters being drawn.

'I imagine anyone would be upset,' Sally said carefully. 'I mean, the child's neglected. . .'

'Yes, but why should Rob especially be upset?' Meg persisted. 'I mean. . . Am I imagining things here?'

The surgeon bit her lip. She crossed to the sink and started washing, waiting until the rest of the team had left the room before she spoke again. Then she shrugged into the soap-suds.

'I guess. . . Look, what I know is old gossip, Meg— stories from when I wasn't even living in the district.

What I know I could easily have wrong.

'All I can tell you is that, no, you're not imagining it, and if you care, Meg Preston—as I'm starting to think you may care by the way you speak of Rob Daniels and the way Rob looks at you—then maybe you should ask him yourself. The stories I know I've never heard from Rob. He tells no one. He speaks to no one about his past before I knew him. And maybe. . .maybe it's time he did.'

Which was all very well, Meg thought crossly as she sat silently beside Rob on the way back out to the farm— but how to broach the subject of shadows with a man who'd plainly put whatever was troubling him firmly behind him?

She couldn't.

It wasn't Meg's place to speak. Nor did she want to be even more emotionally entangled with this man than she already was, she decided, staring fixedly ahead and trying as best she could to avoid the look of trouble on Rob's face. She'd walked out of the hospital to find a silent Rob waiting for her in the car park, and he'd been silent ever since. She mustn't probe somewhere she could only cause pain by entering.

'Are there any of Holly's hens left alive?' she asked tentatively, and the look of tension didn't ease on Rob's face.

'One,' he said shortly. 'I found her in the broody box. The rest. . . Well, if they were still alive I had to destroy them. They were too badly damaged to live. The damn thing killed fifteen hens.'

'And the dog?' Meg swallowed as his look of tension increased.

'I had to put him down.'

'He was vicious.'

'Yeah.' Rob shook his head. 'I anaesthetised him with

a tranquilliser gun to move him from the back door, but it was no use letting him regain consciousness. He's a thoroughly vicious animal, though you can't blame the dog for what he's become. He belongs to the old man you saw—the next-door neighbour.

'Charlie Hann neglects his animals ninety per cent of the time, and I'm about to launch a legal fight to have him declared unfit to keep them. The dog you saw won't have been fed for months. This, though... Well, he wasn't killing because he was hungry. He was killing for the sake of killing, and when a dog's gone that far then there's no choice. He has to be put down. And after its attack on Holly...'

'No. There was no choice,' Meg said firmly, and as she watched the shadow across Rob's face she broke her resolution. She placed a hand on Rob's arm and saw his face tighten as she did so. 'Rob, you were right. You had to put him down.'

The shadow didn't move.

'Rob, what is it?' Meg asked softly. The pain suddenly was unbearable on this face that usually held so much laughter. 'A child's been bitten, some hens have been killed and a dog's had to be put down. It's been dreadful, but there's no real tragedy here. Holly will be fine.

'Hopefully her parents will take better care of her now and maybe...maybe it will even work to her advantage. Sometimes it takes a nightmare to jolt parents into knowing just how much their children mean to them.'

'Yeah, and sometimes even a nightmare's not enough,' Rob said savagely. He caught himself then, looked across at Meg and managed a rueful smile. 'I'm sorry, Meg. It's just... There are echoes here that make me feel...' He shrugged. 'Well, what's past is past. It's only that the past has a habit of shoving its nose in when you least want it. I didn't want it today.'

The past...

The shadows.

'Do you want to talk about it?' Meg asked slowly. There was no choice now whether to ask or not. She hadn't wanted involvement in this man's shadows but she was involved for all that. Somehow involvement had happened the moment she'd crossed Rob Daniel's path.

Rob flicked a glance to her face—and the pain washed from his expression as if he'd caught himself and corrected his features in a way that was more satisfactory.

'I don't much want to talk about it,' Rob said slowly. 'Not now. But thanks for asking, Meg. It was brave of you.'

Meg's eyes flew to his. His voice now held a trace of cynicism and she saw that cynicism reflected in his eyes.

'Rob. . .'

'You didn't want to ask what the trouble was, did you, Meg?' Rob said gently and the cynicism faded, to be replaced by the weariness Meg was beginning to recognise. 'No one really wants to know things that aren't their business. To get involved. . . That's what we're all like really, isn't it? We keep to our side of the road unless we're dragged, screaming, to the other side to pull off some battered creature needing help. Like you were dragged into your cousin's affairs.'

'You seem to get yourself involved without too much kicking and screaming,' Meg said quietly, abashed. Rob's accusation that she hadn't wanted to be involved was too close to the truth for comfort. He saw too darned much, this man. 'You helped us. . .'

'Yes, but that's for my own personal interest.' The weariness broke for an instant with a trace of a smile that faded as fast as it had appeared. 'Or rather it was, until I realised how damned futile it was.' He sighed.

'Look, Meg, why I'm concerned about Eve is because of my past. Once upon a nightmare I let someone down who depended on me utterly, and I thought, well, I thought by helping Eve I could alleviate some of my guilt. I also thought for a stupid few hours that I could share. . . But it hit me. . . It hit me as soon as I realised the depth of what I'm feeling for you. . .I have no right to tear you away from a solid relationship and ask you to love someone like me.'

'Rob. . .'

'Meg, don't worry.' Rob's attention was now all on the road and his face was expressionless. 'I thought. . . Look, somehow I seem to have made a really stupid blunder. Of course you're engaged to your Paul. I've only known you since yesterday. I thought. . . This morning I had a crazy idea that things were suddenly right with the world. The way I felt could only be reciprocated and. . .'

'And what?' Meg took a deep breath, her heart suddenly leaden. Rob was starting to sound sensible—but the nonsensical part of Meg was suddenly unsure whether she liked the new approach.

'Look, let it be, Meg,' Rob said wearily. 'I'm sorry. I'm sorry I pushed you so hard. I'm sorry I kissed you, if you like. You don't want involvement in my past, Meg, and suddenly today I realised that it wasn't fair to try and burden you with it. You can't escape the past. You don't want mine—and what basis is that for a relationship?'

'No basis at all,' Meg managed stiffly.

'Well, there you go, then,' Rob told her. 'End of story. Now. . .let's just get on with it, shall we?' He dredged up a smile, striving for lightness. 'After all, I wouldn't mind betting your beloved Paul is bigger than me. And I'll just bet he's capable of violence.'

With amazement, Meg heard laughter resurface in Rob's voice.

Rob's laughter was a shield, Meg realised suddenly. This man used laughter to protect himself against pain.

To protect himself against a world which had hurt him in some way Meg didn't know.

'I'm. . .I'm sure Paul isn't violent,' Meg whispered, striving to match Rob's laughter. For the life of her she couldn't think how else to react. 'But. . .if you like, I'll see if we can't drum up a few Mafia connections with white socks and concrete shoes.' She took a deep breath. 'Rob. . .'

'Be serious?' Rob threw Meg a cynical look, his laughter fading. 'Is that what you were going to say, Meg? You don't really want me to be serious, though, Meg, do you?'

Did she? Did she have the courage to say, Stop the car, Rob Daniels; I love you and I want to know and love away your shadows?

Of course she didn't.

'I. . .I guess I don't,' Meg agreed bleakly. But, for the life of her, Meg couldn't stop her voice from sounding forlorn as she said it.

They were met at the farm gate by Eve on horseback.

The truck had barely turned off the road before Meg's cousin came galloping over the paddock, her hair flying wildly out behind her and her normally pallid face flushed with exercise and enjoyment. At her side was another youngster—a girl of her own age, also on horseback—and they pulled to a halt at the gate-side, laughing and breathless and very much together.

'You've been ages,' Eve accused, swinging down from her horse and pulling the gate wide for them to enter with an ease that showed that she was a farm girl through and through. Ignoring Meg's open-mouthed astonishment, Eve burbled happily on. 'Lisa and I have been waiting and waiting. Meg, this is Lisa Maitland. The horse I'm riding is called Brandy and Lisa's riding Chesty. Aren't they gorgeous?'

'Gorgeous,' Meg agreed. Meg hardly noticed the horses, though. Her eyes were totally on Eve. The girl's face was suffused with colour. She was as lit up as Meg had ever seen her and, apart from her pathetically thin body, any onlooker could hardly have said that there appeared to be anything wrong with her.

For the first time since Meg had found Eve, she felt a flicker of hope that her young cousin could recover. This was an Eve that other people had told her existed but whom Meg herself had never seen.

'Is something wrong?' Eve asked curiously, and Meg caught herself. She'd climbed from the car and now stood staring at her young cousin, unshed tears glinting under her lashes.

'N—no,' Meg managed. 'I. . . Eve, I didn't know you could ride.'

'Of course I can ride,' Eve laughed. 'I can ride better than I can walk or run. And, Meg, Lisa says her dad told her you've agreed to staying here for a month. A month, Meg! And if Rob says we may stay on the farm till then. . .'

Rob, too, had unwound his long legs from the Land Rover and was standing in the sun, smiling at Eve's eagerness.

'Brandy's been getting fat.' He smiled. 'You can pay for your keep by exercising my horses.'

'I can. . .?' Eve's eyes shone. 'Oh, Meg. . .'

Oh, Meg, indeed. Meg looked at her cousin's sparkling eyes and felt trapped. Trapped by the inevitability of what was happening. Trapped by kindness and care and. . .

And by Rob Daniels' shadows.

'Meg, you do want to stay, don't you?' Eve asked anxiously. 'Lisa says the hospital really needs you.'

'My dad says you're the answer to a prayer,' Lisa informed Meg from her high position on Chesty's back. Meg looked up curiously at Struan Maitland's adopted daughter. Lisa was a pert, cheerful teenager, with blonde hair cut into a neat bob, dancing blue eyes and a sign emblazoned across her T-shirt proclaiming No FEAR.

'Dad says Eve can come to school with me, if she likes,' Lisa continued happily, and Eve grinned up at her, accepting the compliment of proffered friendship with real pleasure.

'We. . . We'll think about it,' Meg said desperately. Things were going way too fast here. Eve certainly couldn't go to school yet—her body's immune system was so damaged by her starvation diet that even a cold could do drastic harm. 'If Eve gains a little weight, maybe. . .'

'Well, I'll do that for sure,' Eve promised, swinging herself back into the saddle with practised ease. 'Maggie has scones for afternoon tea, and she said as soon as we saw you come we had to ride up and tell her to stick them in the oven. So we're off. Scones in ten minutes, guys, and I promise I'll eat three.'

And the girls were gone—a blur of streaming hair and mane and hooves cantering back over the paddocks in a short cut to the house. Meg was left with the sound of their laughter, carrying back to them on the sea breeze.

And with Rob.

'I. . .I don't believe it,' she said faintly, her eyes still following the distant horses.

'Believe it, Meg,' Rob told her, his expression sympathetic. 'What you're seeing is the miracle this place is famous for. Sea-mist healing. All you have to do is relax and let it do its worst.'

'But. . .'

'Without buts,' he told her. 'No buts, Meg. Just acceptance. Acceptance and love—and anything can happen. Just wait and see.'

'It's not working for you.' Meg's voice was almost a whisper, but Rob heard.

'I guess it may be,' he said softly, almost as if talking to himself. 'Maybe. . .maybe I just haven't given it enough time. But maybe. . . Maybe for me even a lifetime isn't long enough.'

CHAPTER ELEVEN

WHAT followed was the strangest period of Meg Preston's life.

On the surface life was absolutely mundane. Only Meg seemed to find life extraordinary. Eve, Maggie and Rob acted as if Eve and Meg had been living on the farm all their lives.

Meg couldn't act like that. What was between Rob and herself was weird, and it was all she could do to sit at the same dinner table as Rob, much less speak to him.

Rob was better at putting past emotion aside than she was, it seemed. The way Rob was acting it was as if the time on the beach—the passion between then that had seemed so strong at the time—was to be forgotten. Rob held himself distant, using laughter and gentle mockery to form a barrier between himself and Meg—or between himself and whatever demons were driving him.

There must be demons, Meg acknowledged, and she ached to know what they were. But Rob's demons were none of Meg's business. She was marrying Paul. While she was engaged to Paul she had no business attempting to reach Rob's barrier of pain—and unleashing who knew what in the process.

Thankfully, Meg's work at the hospital kept her busy.

Her medical role at Gundowring Hospital was also very, very rewarding. Within days Meg could see results from her demand that the entire nursing-home staff shared her concern for patient welfare. Patients who'd been bedridden for weeks—or even months—were being dressed and encouraged to sit in the sun-room or outside on the headland or beach. Those already mildly active were encouraged to join in a number of suggested activities, and the card pack was in danger of gathering dust.

The nursing staff, at first suspicious, had come on side and were now right behind Meg in coaxing, cajoling and downright bullying patients to move. Mrs McKechnie was back playing her piano. Mr Simpson was so well that he was due to be discharged at the weekend, and there was activity and enjoyment in the nursing home now that hadn't been there for a long, long time.

Meg found pleasure in her general practice as well. During the days that followed Meg watched with satisfaction as Holly Edwards recovered quickly from her emotional trauma and her dog bites, and Meg counselled Holly's parents with even more pleasure. Holly's mother made an appointment with Meg the morning after the drama with the dog—ostensibly to thank her—but had burst into tears on her consulting desk.

'I'm just. . .I'm just so ashamed, Doctor. We. . . My husband and I hadn't really wanted a baby and Holly, well, she's been put last all her life. We didn't think. . . Until yesterday we didn't realise just how much she meant to us. And we nearly lost her. Dr Daniels has been so good—so understanding—but he says we need to talk to you. Will you tell us how we go about making up for lost ground? We need to operate as a family and we don't know how. . .'

Dr Daniels has been so good. . .

Just what role was Rob playing in this family drama? Meg thought curiously as she replayed the woman's words in her mind. She made some enquiries and referred both parents to a family therapist, and that night over dinner she told Rob what she'd done. Rob received her news noncommittally but Meg had the pleasure of seeing some of the shadows around his eyes recede.

That had been one of the short personal conversations she'd had with the man. Meg kept herself busy, and when

Rob came into the room at any time she was there she'd excuse herself in a hurry and leave.

Rob did the same to her.

It was easy enough to avoid Rob when he seemed to want the same—but for Meg it was all just so hard.

Between Rob and Meg's young cousin, however, there was no such constraint. Meg watched friendship grow between Rob and Eve with a feeling that was close to jealousy. Rob took Eve wherever he went on his rounds of the local farms, and Eve blossomed with busyness. Surrounded by Rob's dogs and clutching Spud in her arms as if she'd never let him go, at any given time it was Rob who knew where Eve was and not Meg.

It therefore shouldn't have caused her such a shock when, a few days after starting work, Meg walked into Mrs McKechnie's room at the nursing home to find the old lady, Eve, Rob Daniels—and *Spud*—all deep in conversation.

Spud had hardly been out of Eve's arms since the intravenous line had been removed. Now the recovering pup was in another pair of arms. Mrs McKechnie was holding him and laughing and crying all in the same breath as Spud almost turned himself inside out in ecstatic delight.

'Oh, Dr Preston,' the old lady managed through dog licks as Meg entered. 'Your Eve has found my Spud. And Dr Daniels says it's all down to you. He says you and Eve saved his life. I thought. . .I thought the animal welfare people took him when I was admitted here. Dr Cooper said they would. But it seems my little Spud's been wandering, with no one to look after him.

'I can't bear to think about it, but now. . . Now your Eve says she wants to keep him and I can see she's a dear child and she loves him already. . .'

Meg looked wonderingly across to a radiant Eve. So. . .

It seemed that things had been taken out of her hands. Solved without her trying.

And Rob was watching Meg with his face half smiling—the barrier of laughter still drawn.

'That's. . .that's lovely,' Meg managed stiffly. 'I'm. . .I'm just. . . Excuse me, will you please? I. . .I have things to do.'

She escaped. Four pairs of eyes stared after her in astonishment as tears welled up behind her own.

'Meg, what is it with you? It's almost as if you don't like Rob,' Eve complained that night. After visiting Mrs McKechnie, Eve had gone with Rob this evening to visit the recuperating Holly Edwards at home and to place a clutch of fertile eggs under Holly's surviving hen. She was looking tired now, Meg thought, despite being bullied early to bed, but Eve had been bubbling about Rob's mission of mercy. With luck, within weeks Holly Edwards would have a poultry flock again.

Now, tucked into bed by a concerned Meg, Eve hugged her disreputable Spud close and fixed Meg with a look.

'Why don't you like Rob, Meg? I think he's the best thing since horses were invented.' She tickled Spud under the nose. 'Or dogs.'

For Eve that was praise indeed and it was praise well earned, Meg acknowledged. For the past few days, as Meg had worked at the hospital, Eve had spent her time traipsing over farms, delivering calves, holding animals while Rob treated them and generally forgetting her own misery in the all-absorbing excitement of Rob's work. She'd also, unnoticing, gained a little weight!

'I do. . .I do like Rob,' Meg said slowly. 'I just don't. . .'

'Trust him?' Eve asked perceptively. 'Or is it maybe that you don't trust you, Meg Preston?' Eve giggled, the silly childish giggle of a normal teenager which was being heard more and more from her as her stay at Rob's farm progressed. 'I think I'll write to Paul myself and warn him what's happening. Boy, Meg, how can you sit at home and write letters to boring old Paul when you could be bucketing round the country with a hunk like Rob Daniels?'

How, indeed?

Crimson-faced, Meg collected Spud to take him back to his heated bed in Rob's surgery, and bade her cousin goodnight with her dignity still marginally intact. She carried Spud quickly through Rob's surgery—quickly because Rob was there, tending an old Labrador he'd operated on for a bowel obstruction that afternoon. Rob bade her a curt goodnight as she left fast to head for bed.

Bed. . . Meg could put herself to bed without any trouble, but it wasn't so easy to put herself to sleep. She hauled her quilt up to her nose and glared at the ceiling. She had been cross with herself this evening—cross because she'd wanted to go with Eve and Rob so badly that it had been almost physical torture to turn her back on them and write to Paul instead. Now she was cross because Eve was so perceptive. Cross because Rob was in the same house.

Cross because she was jealous of an old Labrador who had Rob with him.

Drat the man. Drat, drat, drat. . .

An hour passed. Another. Still no sleep. Meg rose and padded through to the bathroom between her bedroom and Eve's to fetch a glass of water. Anything rather than stare at the ceiling any longer. She turned on the tap— and then turned it off again to listen.

She wasn't mistaken. There was a harsh cough, muffled but unmistakable, coming from the next room.

Meg threw open the adjoining door. By the light from the bathroom she could see Eve hunched over in bed, coughing into the bedclothes.

'Oh, Eve. . .'

Meg flinched in dismay at the sight of her obviously distressed young cousin—and at the sound of her. She had feared this so much. Weight loss on its own wouldn't kill Eve, but her natural defences were so diminished. . .

Eve's face appeared above the sheet. She choked on another cough and then looked pleadingly up at Meg.

'I'm sorry, Meg. I didn't want to disturb you.'

'Goose.' Meg crossed to sit on the bed and take her cousin's hand. She winced as she lifted the thin fingers. Eve's body was hot to the touch. 'I was still wide awake, Eve, love,' she whispered. 'What's wrong?'

As if she didn't know. . .

'N-nothing. It's just my chest. It hurts. . .'

'And how long has it been hurting?' Meg demanded, her heart jolting with fear. Meg flicked on the bedside light and looked more closely into Eve's face. She'd been right this afternoon in thinking that the child looked paler than usual, and there were now beads of sweat on Eve's thin face.

Eve's cough was dry and harsh. Perching beside Eve on the bed, Meg took both Eve's hands in hers. 'Eve, tell me,' Meg ordered, 'how long has your chest been hurting? Tell me, love. I can't help if I don't know.'

'I just. . .I just felt a bit unwell this afternoon. Just tired, but nothing to worry about. I wasn't going to miss out on taking Holly her eggs, and I didn't want to tell you. . .I didn't want to worry you. . .'

Like Meg, Eve knew the implications. She'd been suffering from pneumonia when Meg first met her.

'It's hurting badly now?' Meg asked, and Eve nodded.

'Like. . .like crazy,' she confessed. 'And it. . .it's hard to breathe and I have such a headache. But, Meg, I'm not going to hospital. I'm not. I'm staying here, Meg.'

'OK.' Meg squeezed her hands as her thoughts raced. 'We won't take you to hospital tonight. You'll need a chest X-ray in the morning so we'll have to take you into town then, but we won't panic yet. Let's get you something for the pain and we'll get some penicillin on board straight away.'

'I can't get sick now,' Eve whispered. 'I've been eating.'

For her entire stay at the farm Eve had been eating without making herself ill, but still she wasn't capable of eating normal, healthy amounts. She'd been looking better—but there was so far to go. . .

'Lie still and try not to cough more than you can help,' Meg ordered, her mind twisting over what had to be done and whether she was crazy not to pick Eve up and rush her to hospital. 'I'll be back in a moment.'

She walked to the door—and Rob was waiting in the passage beyond.

Rob was still dressed from his day's work. Meg and Eve, it seemed, went to bed long before Rob permitted himself to rest. Or maybe, Meg thought perceptively, the shadows didn't allow much sleep.

'Eve's ill?' Rob snapped out the question almost before the bedroom door was shut behind Meg. His voice was laced with raw fear and Meg looked wonderingly up into his concerned face in the dim hall light.

'She's having a bout of coughing and she's running a fever. I think. . .I'm not sure. . .'

'You're worried about pneumococcal pneumonia,' Rob said savagely and Meg's wonder increased. Rob sounded as if he knew Eve's illness well. It seemed that he knew what the disease, anorexia nervosa, entailed and he knew what to expect in the way of complications. And, as well as knowing what to expect, Rob sounded as though he cared very, very much. Almost as if Eve was *his* cousin. Or his child. . .

'Rob, I need some things from my bag,' Meg told him, her voice softening. Instinctively she was treating Rob as she would a relative who was fearful for a loved one. 'My stethoscope's there and I need syringes and penicillin. I think I'll start fluid intravenously as well, just to be sure.'

'You don't want to take her to hospital?'

'Not until morning,' Meg said dubiously, glancing at her watch. Midnight. Not so very long to wait until day-break—and the fright of an emergency trip to hospital in the middle of the night might do more harm to Eve than good. Especially as Meg could start the penicillin and fluids now and watch her herself. 'I. . . My bag's in my car.'

'I'll fetch it,' Rob said grimly, his eyes on Meg's face. 'It's a gamble, not taking her to hospital.'

'I don't think so. I've thought it through and I can cope.' Meg told him what her reasons were and Rob nodded slowly in agreement.

'OK,' he said, and there was no sign of his customary laughter now. 'But you're not alone, Meg. There are two of us to keep watch.'

'There's no need. . .'

'There is a need,' Rob said roughly. 'My God, you have no idea how much there is a need. . .' He broke off, his voice faltering with emotion, and he took moments to collect himself. 'Is there anything else you want?'

'If I can borrow an electric frypan from the kitchen I'll set some steam into the room. It'll ease her breathing,' Meg said slowly, watching his face with care. She felt as if she was stepping on eggshells she couldn't see. She could only feel. 'I'll. . .I'll set up an intravenous drip here. Eve will have to go to hospital in the morning— we can't keep a constant watch here if you and I are to work—but I can get things started now.'

'I'll bring what you need,' Rob said tightly. 'You stay with her.'

Meg nodded. 'Thanks, Rob.'

But he was gone.

An hour later Eve still wasn't asleep and by that time Meg was thoroughly anxious. Her stethoscope told her that there was already congestion in Eve's chest. The infection was moving fast.

'I'm not going to hospital,' Eve whispered over and over again as Meg administered penicillin, set the intravenous drip going and propped Eve up on pillows to ease her breathing. 'I'm not leaving here. I'm not.' She started to cry in distress and Meg stooped and gave her a quick hug.

'There's no need for hospital tonight, love. If we take you tomorrow then I promise I'll bring you home here just as fast as I can. But you mustn't cry, Eve. It'll make your breathing harder and make you cough more.'

'I can't stop.'

'You'd better.' It was a growl from the door and Meg looked up to find Rob re-entering the room. He'd disappeared after bringing what Meg required, realising that she was totally competent to do what had to be done, but now he was back—and in his arms he carried Spud. The dog's floppy ears and feathery tail hung over Rob's arms like a feather duster—a feather duster that wriggled with delight at being allowed back to his favourite spot.

'Spud wondered whether he could help,' Rob smiled, crossing to the bed and placing the small dog on the bedclothes in the crook of Eve's arm. The mutt had been washed and brushed, but he was still as scruffy a dog as Meg had ever seen. 'Spud was wide awake when I went to check,' Rob told Eve gently, watching the traces of exhaustion on the child's thin face. 'He wondered if you'd mind him settling to sleep on your bed.'

Spud might be a disreputable mutt but he certainly seemed to know what was expected of him. He turned one tight circle within Eve's arms, settling himself deep within the bedclothes, raised his face to give the child's wet face a slurpy kiss and composed himself to sleep. Eve's tears turned off like a tap and she even managed a weak smile of pleasure.

'Now, don't you move or you'll disturb him,' Rob growled. 'He needs his convalescent sleep as much as you, Miss Eve, so be good.'

Eve gave a watery sniff, coughed again and looked down at her dog.

'I can't. . .I can't leave him to go to hospital.'

'I should think not,' Rob told her. 'Your duty is to stay right where you are, close your eyes and get you and your dog better. That's an order, young lady. See you do it.'

He gave Meg a small, reassuring smile and turned and left—and moments later Eve drifted into an exhausted and feverish sleep.

Meg sat on alone.

Dog and child slept fitfully but surely and there was little for Meg to do but sit and think.

Think of Eve's health. How she couldn't succumb to pneumonia. Not now.

Think of Rob Daniels' kindness. His concern. His shadows.

Think and think and think. . .

She couldn't think for ever. An hour later, her head spinning in dizzy circles, Meg left the room in search of a cup of tea. A reception committee was waiting in the kitchen.

Meg had half expected Rob to be awake and anxious. That was partly the reason she'd finally left Eve's side— to check that he wasn't waiting up and to persuade him that he, at least, could go to bed.

She hadn't expected the rest of the reception committee.

Paul. Her fiancé. . .

Meg stopped in the doorway to the kitchen, her face blank with shock. For a moment she thought she must be imagining Paul's presence.

She'd done nothing to make herself look more respectable. Meg stood stock-still, her curls disordered around her face after her fight to sleep an age ago—and her sleeveless cotton nightgown her only covering.

Both men rose as Meg appeared in the doorway.

This was no figment of her imagination. It really was Paul.

If Meg was wide-eyed with shock then the immaculately suited Paul was practically gaping. He'd never seen his neatly ordered fiancée in such disarray.

'Meg. . .'

'Paul.'

For a moment shock held Meg numb, and then suddenly the fear of the night—the terror for her cousin—and the sight of this large, reassuring presence from the world she'd left was overwhelming. She stepped forward and placed her arms round Paul's neck—and burst into tears.

Had Paul enfolded Meg in comforting arms, taken her to him and soothed her as she needed to be soothed then her engagement to the man could be seen as being inviolate.

Instead, Paul let his outrage take precedence.

His arms held Meg but they held her back, pushing her away from him so that he could see the ravages of her face and the wildness of her hair.

'Meg, what on earth do you think you're playing at?'

Paul's demand was like a douche of cold water falling over her, and Rob took a hasty step forward.

And stopped. Rob's face twisted into an expression of disgust, then became calmer and coolly watchful.

'Oh, Paul. . .' Meg took a jagged breath and fought for control. She put a hand up and wiped tears from her eyes. 'I just didn't. . .didn't expect. . . You've come all the way from England. Wh-why?'

'Because I couldn't make a word of sense from your phone calls,' Paul snapped. 'You said Eve wasn't sick— and now this. . .this vet. . .' he said the word as if the three letters represented some form of repulsive insect, as he motioned to Rob '. . .this vet tells me that Eve probably has pneumonia. For God's sake, Meg, don't you have any sense at all? And why the hell aren't you dressed if you're wandering round a stranger's house?'

'There's. . .' Meg hiccuped, took another breath and dragged herself back under Paul's hold. 'There's no need to swear at me, Paul.'

'It seems there's every need,' Paul threw back at her. 'I think you've lost your senses, Meg. Get yourself decent while I phone and see if I can discover how we get the kid into hospital. That is, if this God-forsaken hole runs to a hospital that can care for a kid as pathetically sick as your cousin.'

Meg counted to ten. Then another ten. Slowly she drew herself completely away from Paul's arms.

'The hospital here is excellent,' she managed, keeping a hold on her temper with a Herculean effort. 'I told you that on the phone, Paul. But Eve's not going to hospital tonight. I'll take her in tomorrow to have X-rays and if she agrees and it doesn't upset her too much she'll stay there for a couple of days, but tonight I'll take care of her here.'

'Oh, yes?' Paul grimaced. 'You and your mobile intensive care unit, I suppose. Meg, you know damned well she should be in hospital.'

'I know that,' Meg said steadily. 'But I also know she's frightened and she hates hospitals—and I also know Eve's just starting to trust me. I told her I'd take care of her here until morning so that's what I'll do, Paul.'

'And stay up all night? Exhaust yourself in the process?'

'Meg's not alone here,' Rob interjected quietly. He cast a considering glance at her, before looking back to Paul. 'I'm happy to help. And Meg tells me you're a doctor too, Paul. You're welcome to stay here and help as well.'

'Oh, for heaven's sake. . .' Paul spread his hands as if he were talking to two particularly stupid children. 'If Meg thinks I'm sitting up all night, watching a kid whose rightful place is in hospital, she has another think coming.

'I've just spent twenty-four hours on the plane and another five hours in a hire car. I'm exhausted and I intend to sleep, even if you don't. I've booked into the hotel in town and that's where I'll take you, Meg, as soon as you're dressed and we can get your cousin where she should be. Now don't be stupid, girl. Go and get yourself organised.'

'I can't leave now, Paul,' Meg stammered. 'Not when I've promised Eve. You must see. . .'

'I don't see anything,' Paul retorted. 'This is ridiculous behaviour, Meg. The child will do as she's told. Besides, you must see it's totally improper for you to be staying here with this. . .this. . .'

'Vet,' Rob supplied helpfully. 'And might I add— Paul—that I'm very respectable—and I haven't ravished Meg once yet.' He gave a lopsided grin. 'Much as I'd have liked to.'

Laughter! That was all Meg needed. She glared across at Rob and then put her hand to her eyes. She felt dizzy. 'Rob, don't. . .'

'OK, Meg.' Laughter faded as Rob's mouth set in a firm line. 'Enough.' He turned to face Paul, his look calmly set against Paul's furious belligerence. 'Discussion of my respectability can wait until morning. Meg, I'll go in and sit with Eve while you sort out what you want to do. Paul, you're welcome to stay here, if you wish.'

'I'm not!'

'You are welcome,' Rob said gently. 'But if you'd rather not stay here then I'll bid you goodnight.' He held out his hand, took Paul's in his—despite the other man's obvious reluctance—and shook it in a definite gesture of farewell. 'Meg, when you've finished with Paul, make yourself a cup of tea and come back to Eve's bedroom when you're ready. I'll call you if there's any change.'

And Rob walked out and closed the kitchen door behind him.

Meg was left, facing a baffled and furious Paul.

'Meg. . .'

Meg couldn't think. Her almost overwhelming compulsion was to bolt after Rob—but that was a coward's way out.

'Maybe. . .maybe you'd better go back to your hotel until morning, Paul,' Meg managed wearily. 'You. . .you must be tired after your flight. I wish you'd told me you were coming. There was no need to come all this way.'

'Of course there's a need,' Paul said crossly. 'Now I see what a mess you've got yourself into. . .'

'I'm not in a mess,' Meg whispered. 'Believe it or not, things are good. At least, they were until Eve became ill, and there's just as much danger of that wherever she is.'

'If she's dying she's better off dying at home in England,' Paul retorted. 'At least then she doesn't have the power to throw your life into chaos.'

'She hasn't thrown my life into chaos. At least. . . Eve herself hasn't.' She closed her eyes, searching for words. 'Paul, what Eve's been through, well, it's enough to make anyone ill and at heart she's a courageous and loving little girl.

'All I'm doing. . . All I'm doing is loving her, and if my life is in chaos then it's because I love her—not because she's making demands on me. If loving Eve means making myself tired because she's ill then that's fine. If it means bringing some misbegotten pup back to England then that's fine too. I'll do what it takes, Paul. I'll do what it takes to have her happy.'

'And you'll expect me to partake of your martyrdom as well, I suppose,' Paul said savagely. 'Do you expect me to take her problems on as my own too?'

Meg looked up into Paul's angry eyes and sighed. This was hopeless. She should have seen how hopeless the situation was long before this—before he'd come all this distance. 'I guess. . .' Then Meg shook her head. 'No, I guess I don't expect you to help, Paul,' she said softly.

What was she saying, for heaven's sake?

Meg bit her lip. Her fingers clenched into her palms as she forced her tired mind to think. What was she doing—rejecting Paul like this? She had worked so hard for security. She had worked all her life to gain an excellent medical qualification, a rewarding job and a husband who could complement the security she'd craved all her life. And here she was, about to throw it all away.

Was this the right thing to do? Was it?

Then Meg met Paul's eyes again and she knew with utter conviction that it was. It was the only thing to do. She had a choice here between Eve and Paul, and she couldn't let Eve down.

Because she loved Eve.

Which meant that she didn't love Paul.

One last long look and Meg knew that she didn't. She had loved what Paul represented—solid respectability and dependability—but she didn't love the man himself.

And Paul didn't love her, or he wouldn't be asking her to choose. If he loved her Paul would be big enough to embrace an ill and desolate child and her equally forlorn pup—if they came with the woman he loved. But Paul had done the same as Meg. He'd chosen a partner who fitted around the edges of his neat life. He'd chosen a wife because she wouldn't interfere with what he wanted.

'Paul, I'm sorry,' Meg whispered. 'But I think you have to go.'

'Go. . .?' Paul stared. 'You mean back to the hotel?'

'I mean back to England,' Meg said wearily. She sighed. 'Paul, Eve. . . Eve is my cousin and I can't leave her. I love her and I'll do anything it takes to get her back to health. That means. . .that means I won't be sending her back to boarding school. Not ever. It means I'll be keeping Eve and her pup with me and I'll be looking for a place to live where the dog and Eve can be happy. Not necessarily ordered, Paul, but happy. And I don't think you want to share that with us. Do you, Paul?'

'But I want you,' he exploded. 'I want you. Hell, Meg, when I asked you to marry me I didn't. . .'

'Expect appendages?' Meg smiled. 'No. I know that, Paul, and it's hardly fair of me to throw them at you like this. But when I agreed to marry you I was on my own and it's not just me now, Paul. It's me and Eve and Spud-the-dog. I don't think. . .I don't think you want me on those terms. Not honestly, Paul. Not really.'

'I'll take them, Meg,' Paul managed. His face had sagged a little in shock and Meg found herself for the first time feeling sorry for him. 'I'll do my duty by them. . .'

'I know you will,' she said gently. 'But if you're honest with yourself you'll admit you'd rather not—and, Paul, it would be very hard being dependent on a man doing his duty. I think. . .' Meg had been twisting the ring from her finger as she spoke, and now the massive diamond came free. 'I think it's time we were totally honest with each other. Eve's changed things for ever. She's changed me. And I don't think you want the changed me.

'Go back to England, Paul, and find yourself someone who wants your lifestyle as much as you do. I think. . .I think we'll both be much happier if you do.'

Then, because he still looked stunned, Meg stood on tiptoes and kissed his forehead.

'Thank you for coming to my rescue, Paul,' she said softly, trying to salvage what remained of his pride. 'But. . .Eve and I either sink or swim on our own now, and we'd prefer it this way. You've been. . .you've been wonderful, and you've done your duty but. . .but I think you'll have to leave us.'

Paul took a step backward.

'It's this damned vet, isn't it?' he spat at last.

'No.' Meg met his gaze steadily. 'It's not, Paul.'

'I don't believe you.'

There was no answer to that. Meg wasn't sure whether she believed it herself or not.

'I have done the right thing by you,' Paul said angrily, and Meg could see that he was almost reassuring himself. For Paul, duty was paramount. 'If you want to throw my care back in my face. . .' He took a deep breath, then glanced down at the diamond Meg was holding out. He stared down for a long moment and Meg, who knew him so well, could see traces of relief fighting on his face with hurt pride and wounded dignity.

'I'm grateful, Paul,' she said steadily, 'but. . .but there's nothing else and it's time we faced that.'

'Well. . .' Paul took the diamond and met Meg's look. Relief was growing by the minute, though he was trying very hard not to show it. 'If. . . If there's anything you need. . .'

'I know where you are,' Meg assured him gently. She touched his hand. 'I know you'll always help. Paul, thank you. And I'm very, very sorry.'

'Yes, well. . .' Paul shoved the diamond deep into his pocket and Meg wondered fleetingly how long it would stay hidden. Paul had planned to marry this year—and Paul was never a man to have minor hiccups interfere with his plans. Now he turned to the door but hesitated a moment before opening it.

'You'll not stay here for ever?' he demanded.

'I. . . No.'

'So there's really nothing between you and that. . .that. . .'

'No, Paul,' Meg said, her weariness suddenly flooding back. She moved to close the door behind him as he walked out of her life. 'No, Paul. There's really not.'

The lights of Paul's hire car finally faded into the distance. Meg walked slowly back along the corridor to Eve's bedroom, feeling as if she were moving in a bad dream.

She opened the door. Eve and her dog seemed to be still asleep. Beside the bed Rob sat with patient vigilance. He looked a question at Meg as she entered, then rose without a word and came to her.

It was too much. The tears which had been threatening to fall all night were suddenly freed.

Rob's arms enfolded her as Meg crumpled into a sodden heap on his wide, welcoming shoulder.

CHAPTER TWELVE

ON ABOUT her tenth sobbing hiccup Meg finally managed to pull herself away. Rob let her go, but Meg found a large masculine handkerchief being placed into her hand as she was led forward to one of the two armchairs by the bed.

'I don't. . .I don't cry. I never cry,' she whispered as she was gently propelled into the armchair. She retired into the cushions with a watery sniff. Rob sat beside her and his kindly eyes crinkled into laughter.

'I see that. Very wise. This is just a bad case of hay-fever, then?'

'No.' Frantically, and far too late, Meg fought for dignity and detachment. 'I. . . It's just. . .'

'That your fiancé has gone back to his hotel and you're missing him already?' Rob reached forward and took the handkerchief from Meg's nerveless grasp. As he did he caught sight of her ringless finger. For a long moment he stared down—and then, without a comment, he lifted the cloth and wiped an errant tear from her cheek. 'I can understand your despondency. He seems. . .he seems such a. . .such a. . .'

'Rob Daniels, don't you laugh at me.' Meg thrust his hand away and glared for all she was worth, and to her surprise Rob's smile died.

'OK, Meg,' he said seriously, and there was no hint of laughter in his voice. 'I won't laugh. You're right, of course. There's not much to laugh about in Paul. Now, though, I'd like you to go to bed and let me watch Eve until morning.'

'Me. . .' Meg gasped in astonishment. 'Me? I'm not

going to bed. My place is here, with Eve.'

'I won't sleep, though,' Rob told her gently. 'I need to make periodic checks on my old Labrador so I might as well spend the night here. There's no way I'll sleep tonight.'

'Wh-why not?' Meg was lost and it showed. She looked across at Rob, with bewilderment written right across her features.

'Because I can't.' Rob's voice was flat and definite, precluding all questions. 'Meg, go to bed. I promise I'll call if there's the least change, and I can keep as good a check on the drip as you can.'

'But. . .' Meg shook her head. 'Rob, Eve's my cousin. I don't want you making yourself tired caring for her.'

'I need to do this, Meg.' The flat voice shook with something that Meg couldn't define.

She looked up at him, a thousand unanswered questions crowding in her mind but none of them reaching her tongue. To ask questions was to probe behind the barriers this man had set for himself—and Meg knew that there was pain behind the barriers.

He'd told Paul that he wanted to ravish her—but Meg knew that Rob wanted no such thing. It had almost happened on the beach but then Rob had drawn back. He was afraid of crossing barriers. He was afraid of exposing his hurts to the world—of asking Meg to share his burden. By allowing Meg close, he did just that. And the pain ran deep.

Well, if Meg probed the pain then somehow she had to be prepared to heal—and there was only one way that this man could be healed. The same way as Eve could be healed. By unconditional love. By commitment that was as deep as it was absolute.

She saw it then as clearly as daylight through glass. She saw Rob's pleasure in her company—his rising awareness of her and then his sudden withdrawal as he realised that Meg had the power to expose what he had so carefully sealed away, even from himself.

You don't want to ask, he'd told her the day Holly had been injured, and what he'd meant was that Meg wouldn't want the repercussions.

She wouldn't want to make the commitment.

Well, maybe she couldn't.

Meg stared down at the naked finger on her left hand and something inside her cringed. She'd just told Paul that she wouldn't marry him. She wasn't ready for anything more.

Or was she?

Not tonight.

For tonight, all that could matter was that Rob was asking to care for Eve, and Meg knew that his offer was absolutely sincere. She also sensed that he'd told the truth when he'd said that he wouldn't sleep if she made him leave.

His shadows wouldn't let him. Those shadows that Meg was afraid to expose.

She rose unsteadily to her feet and looked from Rob to Eve and back again. Spud opened a sleepy eye and wagged a tail in farewell—then settled to the serious business of sleep once again.

'I'll. . .I'll leave you, then,' she said.

'You trust me with her?' Rob queried, and Meg managed a smile.

'Of course I trust you, Rob,' she managed. 'Of course I trust you.' She walked out of the door and closed it firmly behind her before she echoed her second thought. *I just. . .I just don't trust myself to love you.* 'I just don't know whether I'm capable of so much love. . . Of all the love you need.'

Meg had little sleep that night.

Despite Rob's assurances that he'd keep careful watch,

Meg was still deeply concerned over Eve's health. She was still conscious of the child, sleeping just through the connecting bathroom—and also conscious of the man, vigilant by her bedside.

What drove him? What?

Did she really want to know?

Sleep came at last but it was a fitful sleep, interspersed with dreams of Rob's mocking, smiling eyes—eyes that were shadowed at odd times and troubled for a child he hardly knew. The dreams were almost worse than wakefulness, and Meg welcomed daylight with real relief.

She rose at dawn, showered, dressed and slipped back into Eve's bedroom to find that Rob hadn't stirred from his vigil. He looked up and smiled as she entered.

'There's been no change, Meg. Eve's no worse, and she has slept. I hope you have.'

Rob's smile was strained, and his eyes were dark with weariness. Meg's heart wrenched within her.

'Go to bed yourself for a couple of hours,' she said softly, but he shook his head.

'No. There's work to be done before morning surgery. Will you call the ambulance to take Eve into hospital?'

'I think we must,' Meg agreed. 'My car's too small for her to lie down, and we can hardly take her in the back of your Land Rover.'

'She'd fit,' Rob smiled. 'I can squeeze in four sheep. Surely I can squeeze in one skinny teenager.' He smiled down at the bed and Eve saw that her cousin was awake.

She moved swiftly to the bed and took Eve's hand.

'Good morning, love,' she smiled. 'I. . .I shouldn't have been talking about the ambulance before discussing it with you. Eve, about hospital. . .'

'It's OK,' Eve whispered. 'Rob and I talked it over last time I woke up. I know it's sensible that I should go if I'm to get better fast, and that's what I want. To get better fast so I don't miss any more of my stay here. . .' She broke off in a fit of harsh coughing and as Meg motioned that there was no need to continue she sank again into uneasy sleep.

'I'm right, aren't I?' Rob demanded as Eve settled again. 'She's still ill but she's no worse.'

'She doesn't seem to be.' Meg forced herself to smile at him. 'The penicillin should work quickly, Rob. I'd like to get those X-rays done soon, though, and get Struan to see her as well. He's a physician and he has much more experience of pneumonia than I have. Will you ring the ambulance, or shall I?'

'Leave it to me,' Rob said heavily. He walked to the door and then turned to look back. 'Look after her while I'm away, Meg.'

'Rob. . .'

He looked across at her with no hint of laughter in his face. The mask had been pulled back, and it was all Meg could do not to cross the room, take him in her arms and croon words of comfort and love into the dark recesses of his pain.

Instead. . . Rob looked at her with a blank, dull look and Meg held herself tightly under control.

'Yes?' he asked, and Meg shook her head.

She didn't have the courage.

'Don't let your heart rule your life,' Meg's mother had told her over and over again. 'Look where it got me. Into a mess so big I almost went under. If you must marry then marry a man for sound, sensible reasons.

'Know everything there is to know before you commit yourself—and if that requires references in triplicate from every vicar and bank manager from here to Land's End then don't fall in love without them. Don't ever forget that, Meg. Don't let your heart take crazy risks.'

The lesson had been drummed into Meg since she'd been old enough to listen—and now that same lesson held Meg where she was. Afraid to open her arms. Afraid to open her heart.

'I. . . It doesn't matter,' she said dully. 'I just wanted to say thank you.'

'My pleasure,' Rob said in a voice devoid of all expression—and he was gone.

Over the next two days Meg hardly saw Rob.

With Eve settled into the children's ward at the hospital, there seemed little point in Meg returning to the farm at night. Instead, she slept in one of the hospital flats so that she could wedge her hospital responsibilities in with spending as much time with Eve as possible.

It also kept her away from Rob.

Rob kept careful tabs on Eve. His presence at the hospital was intermittent but frequent. With the big glass windows at either end of the children's ward, though, Meg was able to see when he was there and to reschedule her own visits accordingly.

She didn't want to see him. She didn't want to face him.

What was there about Rob Daniels that was making Meg feel more and more of a coward?

Eve spent another twenty-four hours on the danger list and then bounced toward recovery as swiftly as she had fallen ill. It seemed that she hardly had a choice in the matter.

Meg was astounded at the concern shown to her young cousin by all the hospital doctors from the time Rob had called for the ambulance. It seemed that the entire medical community of Gundowring was intent on one thing— bringing Eve to health—and that Meg's medical skills were superfluous.

Meg spent considerable time with Eve, ducking in between seeing her own patients and spending every free moment with her—apart from the times when she found

Rob at Eve's bedside—but, in fact, Meg was hardly needed at all. Nearly every time she entered Eve's ward she found one or other of the town's doctors there, and by the end of two days Meg was starting to believe that Eve was the most overtreated patient she'd ever met.

'Why Eve needs a surgeon visiting her, I don't know,' Meg told Sally when she found the young surgeon at Eve's bedside. 'And Lloyd's been in three times today, that I know of—an anaesthetist, of all things. Gina's been in often and Struan practically lives in the ward. Their daughter Lisa's been hovering like an anxious mother hen, pouncing on me all the time to know what's happening—as well as driving her parents demented with demands to be kept up to date.'

'It's because we all care,' Sally said gently, taking Meg's arm as they walked together toward the nursing home.

'I don't know why you should,' Meg said bluntly. 'We've been here for only two weeks and we've less than two weeks to go before we leave.'

'Yeah, well, I've been meaning to talk to you about that.' Sally tucked Meg's arm into hers more securely. 'Meg, have you thought of staying?'

'Here?' Meg frowned at her new friend. 'For ever, you mean? No. You know my home's in England.'

'Home is where the heart is, Meg, dear,' Sally said gently. 'And I don't think your heart is in England any more. Is it, Meg?'

'Of course it is.' Meg took a deep breath. 'Sally. . .'

'I know. It's none of my business,' Sally agreed. 'But the whole town knows your fiancé came here and booked a room for you as well as for him at the hotel. We also know that despite the double booking only he stayed the night, he stayed alone and he left first thing next morning.

'And. . .' she lifted Meg's unresisting hand and inspected the white bare line at the base of Meg's ring finger '. . .we've also noticed your ring disappeared on the same night. You can't stay in a small town without these things getting noticed, Meg, and so I warn you.'

'It. . . It doesn't matter,' Meg said breathlessly. 'Sally, even if I'm no longer engaged to Paul it doesn't make a difference. I still live in England.'

'But Rob Daniels lives here.'

Meg pulled away with a fierce shrug and glared at her friend. 'Sally, you're out of line.'

'I always am,' Sally agreed cheerfully. 'Ask my husband, Lloyd. He'll tell you I delight in sticking my nose into other people's business and I never butt out when I'm not wanted. Well, Lloyd's a case in point. When I came here he was engaged to someone entirely unsuitable. So I fixed it.'

'What. . .what did you do?' Meg asked, fascinated despite her anger.

'Found someone else for the lady in question to marry, and seduced my wonderful Lloyd, of course,' Sally laughed. 'I practically bustled him to the altar before he knew what had hit him. And very happy I've made him, too. So. . . What about a bit of seducing on your part, Meg Preston?'

'Sally, don't. . .'

'Look, Meg, there's a few things going on here that need to be sorted out,' Sally said bluntly. She stopped dead and placed her hands on her hips, with the air of one lecturing a recalcitrant pupil. She held up one finger. 'Listen.

'One, Rob Daniels is a damned fine vet and everyone here thinks the world of him.

'Two, he's downright miserable. He's shied away from relationships because of what happened to him in the past, but for the first few days you were here it was like a curtain being drawn so we could see the real Rob Daniels. We all thought we were watching a miracle.

'Three, you, Meg Preston, change colour whenever the man comes into sniffing distance and you duck for cover whenever you see him coming. You might think you're hiding your feelings but you're not hiding them from me.

'Four, something's happened between you and Rob to take the happiness out of Rob's step. To destroy our miracle. I don't know what the trouble is but at least now you're rid of your fiancé and are free to take the initiative.

'And, five, you've less than two weeks left to make both of you happy. From the way Rob's looking, he's resigned himself to misery for the next hundred years— so the initiative had better come from you, Meg.'

Sally grinned. 'There. I've said my piece. I'll take off before you vent your anger on yours truly. Go and do a few medico-legal letters while you think about what I've said. I always find writing letters to lawyers a lovely way to vent my spleen. But, Meg, do please think about it. For your own sake, if not Rob's.'

And she took herself smartly down the path before Meg could reply.

Meg stood staring after her, her mouth practically agape.

How on earth could she concentrate after a conversation like that?

She couldn't.

Meg went into her office and did some desultory bookwork, but even a long letter to a lawyer who'd been demanding patient information he had no right to wasn't enough to bring her attention back to medicine. She glanced at her watch. Five. Time to go home.

Back to her hospital flat. And tomorrow back to the farm with Eve. And then. . . Then a few more days until the new locum came to replace her here and she and Eve could go back to England.

Nothing would change in the next few days, Meg

knew. She and Rob had just about perfected this avoidance business. They could live in the same house for two weeks without discussing anything.

Well, that was all right with Meg. She didn't want to discuss anything.

Did she?

Meg sat and stared out of her window to the sea beyond. There were three more hours of daylight, and Meg had finished her work for the day. Now. . . Should she go to the beach to swim? Or be more sensible? Find a medical book and do a little studying? Visit Eve? Have dinner in the hospital kitchen?

Or do something more?

Meg lifted a pencil and balanced it between two fingers.

This is stupid, she thought. Her eyes drifted across to the hospital car park. Rob's Land Rover was there. He'd be with Eve.

In two weeks Meg wouldn't see Rob Daniels ever again.

Which was just how she wanted it, she thought savagely, and she bent the pencil until it snapped. Then she stared down at the splintered ends without really seeing them.

In two weeks she'd be back in England—and the thought was leaving her feeling as bereft as she'd been the week her mother had died. Worse. It was as though something were being torn from her.

'He doesn't want me,' she whispered. 'He doesn't.

'He doesn't know what he wants. He's hurting.

'You can't fix that.

'You can try.

'It's a crazy risk you'd be taking, and you know you don't take risks. . .'

She was talking aloud, and the words were ringing in her ears as a meaningless jumble.

The sea was a blurred expanse of turquoise through the window. The mist had come in for the evening, creeping in with its gentle coolness after the heat of the day. No longer did the searing Australian sun have the power to burn. The mist was settling.

A healing mist. . .

A knock at her open door pulled Meg out of her reverie. She looked up, to find old Mrs McKechnie peering anxiously in.

'I'm not interrupting, am I, dear? I thought I heard someone talking. . .'

Meg hauled herself away from her inner conversation and managed a welcome.

'Just me, Mrs McKechnie,' she smiled. 'I'm talking to the walls. Come in and give me someone a bit more lively to talk to.'

'Well, if you're sure.' The old lady tottered forward and lowered herself thankfully onto a chair. She'd recovered well from her infection but was still weak. 'I just wanted to say. . . Well, I wanted to thank you.' Elaine McKechnie clasped her hands primly before her on Meg's desk. 'If it wasn't for you I'd be pushing up daisies, and I'm very grateful.'

'Mrs McKechnie!' Meg's humour surfaced and she chuckled. 'The daisies will have to stay underground for a lot longer if they're waiting for you,' she smiled. 'And there's no need to thank me. I did what any competent doctor would have done. It was just bad luck that Dr Cooper wasn't what he was supposed to be.'

'I know that, dear,' the old lady told her. She hesitated and then seemed to take her courage in both hands. 'But. . .because of what you've done I decided to talk to you. I'm grateful, and I so hope things are going beautifully between you and your young man. I do so want our young Dr Daniels to be happy. But I'm afraid things aren't going well, are they, dear?'

'Not. . .not beautifully,' Meg said blankly. She took a deep breath. 'But, Mrs McKechnie, Dr Daniels is not my young man.'

'Well, yes, he is, dear,' the old lady said apologetically. 'That is, he is if you want him. You only have to see the way he looks at you to know he's nutty on you, and when he talks about you he goes all soft. He's been in a lot these last couple of days, bringing Spud in to see me when he comes in to visit your Eve.' She sighed.

'Anyway, when Dr Daniels talks about you. . . My Charlie looked at me just like that—and he was nutty on me for fifty years, so I ought to know. And now you've stopped wearing your ring—well, I just thought I might say something because you helped me so much, and if you need a bit of encouragement—well, you weren't backward in helping me, dear.'

'Mrs McKechnie, I don't need encouragement.'

'Maybe not, dear—but he does, and you're the one who has to give it to him. If you can find the courage.'

Meg stared down at her hands. This was a crazy conversation between doctor and patient. She should end it at once. Instead, she looked over at the bright old eyes and found herself asking what she had no business to.

'Mrs McKechnie, why do you think Rob. . .Dr Daniels . . .would need encouragement? He's a grown man. If he wants me. . . If he wants me, then surely. . .' She broke off, blushing to the roots of her hair. What a crazy thing to ask.

Mrs McKechnie, though, was smiling like the wise old bird she was.

'He's got a past,' she said sagely. She settled back in her chair and fixed Meg with a stern look. 'And maybe. . .maybe it's time someone told you what you're up against.'

'So, what am I up against?'

Meg had no business asking the question, but

there was no way she was retracting now.

'His mother, that's who you're up against. And guilt so strong it must be crippling.' The old lady's voice grew bitter. 'Dear, Margaret Daniels was a social climber who had ambitions for her children from the moment they were born. She drove them so hard. . .Robby and Patricia. They were two lovely kids, but nothing they did was right for Margaret.

'If they came home with ninety-nine per cent for a test she beat them for losing one mark. If they went to a dance and didn't dance with the richest kids in the district she'd shame them in public. Haul them off the floor and tell their partners to stick with their own class.

'Rob's father was a mouse of a man. He never stood up to Margaret and she was left to drive the kids to the end of their tether. And she did. Rob won a scholarship to a London university—a great honour—and she boasted and boasted, but what the stupid woman couldn't see was that for Rob it was an escape. At seventeen he was too young to see the consequences of leaving. He walked away and never came back. Until. . .

'Until?'

'Until it was too late,' Mrs McKechnie whispered, and suddenly Meg knew what was coming. She felt horror building in her like a cancer in her heart.

'Patricia just couldn't make it,' the old lady continued sadly. 'When Rob left Pat broke her heart, but that didn't stop her mother's pressure. After a while the child just stopped eating. A normal mother might have contacted Rob—pleaded with him to come home—but no one did. Margaret said he wasn't to be told and I suppose the boy didn't have the money to come home for a visit, even if he'd wanted to. Rob's vet course was for five years.

'He came home to Australia when he was twenty-two to find Patricia so close to death that there was nothing anyone could do. Just watch the end.'

'Dear heaven. . .' Meg whispered. 'Oh, Rob. . .'

'That was the end of his family, as far as Rob was concerned,' Mrs McKechnie continued gravely. 'What the boy said to his parents I don't know but the farm hands said the bitterness was dreadful. He left here the day after Patsy's funeral.

'I heard he was practising his vet medicine in Sydney, but he never came home until his parents were both dead. Even then, we didn't think he'd stay. Not with the ghosts. With his parents' awful marriage and his guilt about Patricia gnawing at him since he was so young, none of us ever thought he could find a permanent, happy relationship. But then you came. . .'

Then Meg came.

Meg lifted her head and looked directly at Mrs McKechnie, and the old lady met her look with honesty and with something else. With a challenge.

Rob. . .

Pain knifed through and through Meg's heart as Rob's shadows clicked into place. His eagerness—his compulsion to help. . . Was that why he had wanted Meg in the beginning—as a way of helping Eve? And then later he'd seen emotional involvement looming and had drawn back in fear. If his sister had loved him and he blamed her death on his leaving. . .maybe he didn't see himself of worthy of being loved again.

Maybe. . .

And all of a sudden Meg knew that she was right. She knew what the shadows were—but how could she fill a need like that?

How could she not?

Meg rose slowly to her feet and stood looking down at Elaine McKechnie's troubled face.

'Thank you for telling me this,' she whispered. 'I guess. . .I guess I needed to know.'

'But will you do anything with it?' the old lady said insistently. 'Will you?'

'I don't know if I can,' Meg admitted. Then she took a deep breath and looked out to where the sea mist was swirling over the ocean. Rob's Land Rover was parked between her and the sea. He was still here. He was here now.

'I don't know if I can,' she repeated. She took a deep breath, and as she did so the fears her mother had instilled in her fell away to nothing. What was the risk Meg was taking, compared to the pain Rob had already suffered? What cost a risk?

She turned back to the old lady, who was watching her with troubled eyes. Gently she reached out and touched the gnarled old hands—a touch that seemed to embrace a love that threatened to overwhelm her.

'I'll try.'

CHAPTER THIRTEEN

WHEN Rob returned to his Land Rover Meg was waiting.

He saw her as he reached the edge of the car park. Spud trotted at his heels after an illicit visit to the children's ward, and he at least bounded forward—on three legs—to greet Meg with delight.

Rob also smiled in greeting but she could see the shutters being drawn. The shield of laughter being raised.

'Meg. Hasn't Struan kept you too busy to be hanging round car parks?'

Rob's eyes slid over Meg's trim form as he spoke. She'd changed swiftly into a simple cotton dress—a favourite of hers with no sleeves, a low-cut neckline and flowing skirt. She'd pulled her hair free and, with bare legs and sandals, looked anything but the doctor she was. Rob's smile died and his face grew tense.

'I was waiting for you,' Meg said resolutely. 'I've put a basket of goodies from the hospital kitchen in the back of your Land Rover. I wondered if you'd take me to your beach.'

'My beach. . .'

'The one you took me to two weeks ago,' she said gently. 'I need a swim.'

'Meg. . .' Rob's face closed up, excluding her completely. 'I can't. I have work to do. Patients to see.'

'Then I'll come with you,' Meg said cheerfully. 'And we'll go afterwards.'

'Maggie already has dinner. . .'

'Maggie has not.' Meg took a deep breath, trying desperately to maintain her courage. 'I rang her to say you wouldn't be in.'

'Meg. . .'

'So you might as well take me.' She smiled and slid into the passenger seat of his vehicle. 'No?'

For a long, long moment Rob stood staring down at the girl in the vehicle, his face reflecting his doubt. Spud, though, had none of Rob's reservations. Ignoring his splinted leg as of no consequence, he bounded onto Meg's lap and looked expectantly up at Rob.

Well? his wagging tail proclaimed. What are we waiting for?

What, indeed?

'I'll do my work afterwards,' Rob said tightly. 'If you must have a picnic. . .'

'I must.'

They didn't speak at all until they reached the beach, and by the time Meg had her picnic spread on the sand her courage was beginning to desert her.

Rob was acting as if he would rather be anywhere in the world but here—with her.

Sally's words and those of Mrs McKechnie kept ringing in Meg's ears, but it took sheer nerve to force herself to stay cheerful. Sheer nerve to spread a rug on the sand, load her plate with salad and chicken from the hospital kitchen, pour wine for both of them and make herself eat.

All the while the soft sea mist swirled around the silent pair. It was a comfort to Meg, seeming to enfold her in its healing power and giving her courage. It didn't have the power to make her happy, though. Only Spud seemed cheerful, chomping his share of chicken and then digging delightedly in the sand and barking at incoming waves.

'He's a changed dog,' Meg said softly as she finally laid down her plate and took Rob's from him to place back in the basket. 'You've given him a new life, Rob.'

'It was you and Eve who've done that,' Rob said

heavily. He rose and stood staring out to sea. 'If you've finished. . .'

'I haven't started.'

'Do you. . .do you want a swim, then?'

'I didn't mean that.' Meg stood too and stepped across the rug to lay a tentative hand on his arm. 'Rob, I made you come here. . .I need. . .I need to talk to you.'

'I don't know why.'

'I think you do,' Meg whispered. 'Rob, I know about Patricia. I know. . . And I want to help so much it hurts.'

'Meg, no!' Rob wheeled around to face her, pulling back out of the reach of her appealing hand. His hands clenched into fists and there was no trace of laughter now. 'Meg. . .' His voice died helplessly away.

It was now or never. Now or never. . .

It had to be now. And, in the end, the words were easy.

'Rob, I love you.' Meg told him, watching pain wash over his face with an echoing pain in her heart. 'I haven't been brave enough to tell you. . .I had my own reasons for thinking that love was something you kept under control—something you divided out when the time was right. But loving Eve has changed on a perceptions on a few things and no. . .loving you has changed everything.

'I love you, Rob Daniels, and I want you to know that if you want me. . . Rob, I know you don't want to commit yourself emotionally, but maybe. . .maybe I have enough love for both of us. Maybe I can keep us going, Rob. Love you, regardless. Keep loving you until. . .until one day you might—'

She broke off, unable to go one word further.

Silence. Rob's face was inscrutable. His expression gave nothing away.

'Rob. . .' Meg's whisper broke and she shook her head in despair. Fought so hard for courage. 'Rob, you said you felt something when you first met me. As if. . . as if we've known each other for so long. . . Well, I feel that, too. I feel like I know you so well.

'I guess. . .I guess you think you'll hurt me if you ask for my love but, Rob, the only way you can hurt me is not to love me now. For better or for worse, I've given myself to you. Don't leave me, Rob. Don't make me go away because I can't bear it.'

There. She had done it. She'd exposed herself to any-thing this man cared to dish out to her. She was wide open to pain.

'You'd do that?' Rob asked blankly, his face expressionless. 'Give yourself to me. . .'

'I don't have to give myself to you,' Meg told him, and the last of her doubts faded as she faced what she was saying as absolute truth. 'I'm already yours, Rob Daniels. I've. . .I've been trying to avoid it. Running away, if you like. But I can't, Rob, because I love you so much that I think I already am a part of you.

'You said it yourself, remember. Back here on the beach. It's as if we've known each other for ever. You saw it too, but when you realised what it involved—that you could never be alone again and your pain was my pain—then you backed away.

'Maybe because you thought you'd be burdening me or maybe—because you loved and lost your sister—you don't want to expose yourself to love again. But. . .but, Rob, your pain is my pain, regardless of whether you love me back. You are. . .you are a part of me and I ache for you and I love you, regardless of what you do with me. Now. . . Now and forever.'

Silence. Absolute silence. Even the sea seemed to quieten. Everything seemed to wait with bathed breath for Rob Daniels' world to shift on its axis.

And it did. Ever so slightly.

He half turned toward her in the mist, and it was enough. Meg took one step forward, watching his face, and what she saw there made her take another.

And then somehow she was no longer in control. It was Rob who was doing the moving forward, reaching for her hands and pulling her into his arms—as if he was unable to believe that she wouldn't disappear into thin air unless he took her to him. As if his hunger for her was somehow overwhelming, and a force stronger than either of them was driving them together and holding them.

'Meg. . . Dear heart. . . My lovely Meg. . .' Rob's voice was a breathless whisper of passion. Unbelieving. . . As if he were seeing a miracle.

And then she had his face between both her hands and she was drawing him down to her to kiss his beloved face. . .to smooth away the pain around his eyes. . .the pain around his heart. . .the pain of years being taken into her heart, moving out again and somehow evaporating high into the lovely sea mist swirling around them.

Two lovers. Man and woman. A passion as old as time, yet more precious than a thousand diamonds.

A man and a woman becoming one.

A kiss to end all kisses. A kiss to heal, to seal and to start again.

A kiss to make them man and wife.

Afterwards. . . When passion finally abated enough for them to draw apart, Meg's world had shifted too. She stood in the enfolding arms of her love and knew that she would never be released.

She looked up and found Rob smiling at her, and at her feet Spud wriggled in ecstatic delight.

It was as if the little dog sensed that his world was also right. He would stay here in this magic place, with his wonderful Eve and with visiting rights to the old lady who still loved him in the nursing home. He would supervise his young mistress's healing, and he'd watch the growth in love and wonder of this man and this woman. He'd watch a family grow from this embryonic love, and maybe he'd even lord it over a few collies in the process. . .

'Meg,' Rob was saying unsteadily. 'Meg. . .'

Meg held her love more tightly. She stood on tiptoe and kissed him softly on his lips. 'Y-yes, my love. . .?'

'You can't. . .' Rob's voice was husky with passion. 'You don't even know anything about me.' He held her at arm's length. 'Meg, you have to know. . .'

'I know as much as I need to.'

'But I need to tell you.' Rob took her back into his arms and his eyes devoured her with a hunger that held her in thrall. 'Meg, you guess so much about me. . . You know. . . And what you guess is right.

'Pat's death left me emotionally dead. My parents' marriage was a cold, passionless affair. They didn't love me and the only love I felt was for Pat. She died, and it was my fault. I was too damned young and selfish at seventeen to see the consequences of my leaving. Pat's death left me feeling as if I never wanted emotional involvement again, but then I met you. . .

'You seemed so sweet. . .so caring. And I knew you were different. When I met Eve and saw Patricia's ordeal being replayed so strongly I thought. . .by being involved with you I could help Eve. But then, when I let myself get close, what I felt scared me to death. It left me wide open. Open to the pain I thought I could never face again. But I guess that's what loving's all about, Meg. . . Exposing yourself. . .'

'I won't hurt you, Rob.'

'You don't have to tell me that,' Rob said in a voice that shook with emotion. 'I just hope to hell I don't hurt you.'

'I trust you not to.'

He stared down at her, and the emotion on his face told her his thoughts. There was wonder there, and love.

And there was healing. Gentle, blessed healing.

And finally there was also the beginning of a smile. Joy swept in like the tide, carrying all before it with a force so strong that it shook them both. With a deep sigh of happiness, Rob swept his Meg up into his arms and held her close.

'You'll marry me, my Meg? I'll brook no half-measures here, my love. You'll marry me, my golden girl? My blessed healer? My love?'

'Of course I'll marry you,' Meg whispered in wonder. 'Of course. Oh, Rob. . .'

'Do we have any bread left, Dr Preston?' Rob demanded suddenly, peering over his love to see into the picnic basket.

The inexplicable demand left Meg confused. For a moment she thought she hadn't heard Rob right, and then had to fight her dazed mind to find an answer. 'Y-yes. . .I think so. . .'

'Good. Pick it up.'

He lowered her so that she was able, wondering, to lift the half-loaf from the basket. Then she lay back in his arms and looked with joy up at her husband-to-be.

'Why. . .why do you want bread?' she asked, and she was suddenly shy. 'Are you. . .are you hungry?' Ridiculous question.

'Nope,' Rob answered and he started striding toward the waves. 'You asked me to take you for a swim, Meg Preston, and you're about to have one.'

'But. . . Rob, I'm still dressed,' Meg squeaked. 'So are you. Put me down.'

'No fear,' he said strongly. 'No way. Not ever. And there's an appointment we have to keep. We really should be in our Sunday best to do this, but this will have to do. Kick your sandals off, Meg, love.' And he kicked his own shoes from his feet and kept right on going, wading waist-high into the waves and further.

'Rob. . . Rob. . .'

Breast-deep, Rob paused, lifted the bread from Meg's still hands as she clung to him and solemnly broke the bread into two pieces.

'This is where we stop, Meg Preston,' he told her gently, and his eyes caressed her without the need for touch. His love was all around, warming her in its entirety. 'I'll meet you underwater.'

'Underwater. . .'

'I'd like to shout it from the rooftops,' Rob said solemnly, 'but for now. . . For now I'd like to introduce my affianced wife to one gentleman cod. And after that. . .after that, the world.'

FREE!

FOUR FREE
specially selected
Medical Romance™ novels
<u>PLUS</u> a FREE Mystery Gift
when you return this page...

Return this coupon and we'll send you 4 Medical Romance novels and a mystery gift absolutely FREE! We'll even pay the postage and packing for you.

We're making you this offer to introduce you to the benefits of the Reader Service™– FREE home delivery of brand-new Medical Romance novels, at least a month before they are available in the shops, FREE gifts and a monthly Newsletter packed with information, competitions, author profiles and lots more...

Accepting these FREE books and gift places you under no obligation to buy, you may cancel at any time, even after receiving just your free shipment. Simply complete the coupon below and send it to:

MILLS & BOON READER SERVICE, FREEPOST, CROYDON, SURREY, CR9 3WZ.

READERS IN EIRE PLEASE SEND COUPON TO PO BOX 4546, DUBLIN 24

NO STAMP NEEDED

Yes, please send me 4 free Medical Romance novels and a mystery gift. I understand that unless you hear from me, I will receive 4 superb new titles every month for just £2.20* each, postage and packing free. I am under no obligation to purchase any books and I may cancel or suspend my subscription at any time, but the free books and gift will be mine to keep in any case. (I am over 18 years of age)

M7YE

Ms/Mrs/Miss/Mr _____
BLOCK CAPS PLEASE

Address _____

_____

_____ Postcode _____

MILLS & BOON®

Medical Romance™

COMING NEXT MONTH

I'D LOVE A BABY! by Margaret Barker

Jenni Dugdale wanted a baby! And Dr Carl Devine offered to father the baby and leave Jenny to bring up the baby on her own. The natural way was surely the best, and Jenni willingly agreed. But then she wanted Carl to stay and play the part of father *and* husband!

DOCTOR'S DILEMMA by Sheila Danton

Serina Grant's holiday in Canada was to help her overcome her mother's death. Then she met Greg Pardoe and the attraction was instant. But he would only have a casual fling and she refused. There was only one solution—but it was all up to Greg...

A SPECIALIST'S OPINION by Lilian Darcy

Summer moved to Bermuda to be with her fiance. But shortly after her arrival the engagement ended. So Summer plunged herself into her work—and that meant close contact with the attractive Randall Macleay. Then he found out why she had broken with her fiancé...

WINGS OF DEVOTION by Meredith Webber
Flying Doctors

Kelly Jackson arrived at the base and announced that she was Colin Forbes, Jack Gregory's new locum! Colin was on his honeymoon and she was his replacement. Jack found Kelly infuriating and intriguing. But they both carried baggage from the past...